The Elders of Arkhide

Cooperative Realm

Nicky Penttila

The Elders of Arkhide

Chapter One

Everyone in the Cooperative Realm thought the planet Arkhide was filled with monsters.

What would they think of this garden, then?

Mondrian Delacroix stepped through the door-field from Arkhide Orbital Station's airless metal corridor into the gorgeous abundance of its garden. Her boots sank softly into the sandy plasticrete flooring. The gentle give stood a stark contrast to the unyielding metal of the rest of the station.

Arkhide Orbital had been built first for synthetic humans, not bags of bones and muscle like Mon.

Why in Safra's name had Aimee Five asked her to come here, anyway?

She knew why.

Heather. It had to be Heather.

Mon pushed back the helmet of her atmosuit, corralled her wayward hair again, and took a deep breath of clean air. The rich loam of actual soil was a novelty sweet enough to awaken childhood memories of long walks with her foster parents.

Heather hadn't been so lucky with her parents. How she'd become Mon's responsibility, though, was all on Mon.

Blasted damsels in distress.

She tried to cast her thoughts toward the sweetness of the new grass and the old roses. The tang of moisture in the light breeze, the dew allowed to linger before being whirred away by the air scrubbers. The foliage, shimmering greens and golds like an emerald tapestry, rustling in the artificial breeze as if greeting an old friend.

Mon's lip twisted wryly. She'd been here only once before, a short eight months ago.

She'd come on a sort of diplomatic, mostly deliriously painful mission, towing seventeen-year-old Heather Quostov along with her like a stray kitten. A seventeen-going-on-thirty, astromechanical genius of a kitten.

With the synthetic humans' help, they'd solved their mystery, and also found a temporary home for Heather. Well, Heather had found it. She'd begged to stay, to dive into all the new tech the synths might show her.

Thank Safra, Arkhide had said yes.

Staying here had saved the girl, for now, from the Cooperative's greedy claws. Heather, like Mon, had an extremely rare skill. They could "hear" certain wavelengths normally far outside normal human range. The perception wasn't just through their ears, but that's how their brains liked to interpret it.

Heather's Listening abilities might be greater even than Mon's. A fact Mon had omitted from the report she sent her Co-op bosses after she'd done the girl's initial screening.

Living in the world was hard when you could sense every machine hum, every power line, every magnetic wave. Most Listeners couldn't really function outside of special environments that offered a lot of accommodation. And a lot of training in self-control—which the Co-op was good at.

And then they owned you.

Until now.

Heather had devised a way to modify noise-canceling headphones to also block nearly eighty percent of the sounds only Listeners could sense.

It was going to change everything.

Now they could choose when to Listen and when not to. And they didn't need the Co-op's help to do it.

Mon slipped off her gloves and dipped a hand into the rich, loamy dirt of one of the flower beds. The cool, moist earth against her skin mirrored its tangible connection to the vibrant life it nourished. Not a Co-op base, for sure.

Heather's invention had helped all the known Listeners in this sector. All one hundred twenty of them.

After Mon mustered out of Cooperative Central Command— her twenty years done done done!—she'd spent the last six months delivering Heather's headsets far and wide. Watching the faces of the people the first time they switched the earphones on was sheer delight.

Arkhide's patent attorneys had ensured Heather's claim before Mon had let the Co-op see the headphones. Now Co-op Central had a license for the tech, and Heather had a passive income.

She would never need to muster in.

No Listener ever would.

Walking slow, avoiding the meeting she wasn't quite late for, Mon trailed her fingertips over the delicate leaves of a nearby vine. Its buds might be berries soon.

Arkhide's sun gave a lot of light to this garden, tucked into one of the two squared-off donuts that made up the space station. Half the garden's outer wall and all the ceiling was clear to space, letting in the light and also giving a fair view of the planet below.

It was a strange angle, not quite center, not quite at the one-third mark. Mon didn't doubt that it was the perfect angle for the light. Synthetic humans surely preferred precision over aesthetics.

Except, look at this garden. All manner of plantings separated into precise squares and triangles of foliage but allowed to be wild within them. Practical vegetable plots across the walk from a riot of pansy-like flowers. Balanced, beautiful, true.

Creepy, how pleasing they'd made it to human senses.

This new patent of Heather's, surely it was just the first of many clever, patentable, things she would devise. She was the perfect kind of person for Arkhide, the system's only world of synths and enhanced humans.

Were the Arkhideans really about to boot her off now? And why did they have to tell Mon that in person?

To collect her and take her away.

Blasted teenage damsels in distress.

Mon rounded a corner, heading toward that clearing in the center with the benches where they'd held the big negotiations. Back when she had a job. A job she never wanted, but at least it had given her a direction. Now, who was she? And who would she be to Heather if the synths decided to send the girl away?

Humans must seem so slow and ponderous to a people who could communicate with one another at the speed of thought. At the speed of multiplexed thought.

She remembered this stand of thick bamboo stalks, backed up to the open space. Focusing on it, and tuning down her Listener sense, blocking the clashing waves of all the mechanisms holding this station together, she could imagine she wasn't on a station at all. But she was, and there was a problem.

As Mon stepped into the tiny diamond clearing, everything stilled for a heartbeat, the very air holding its breath. The familiar woven bamboo benches radiated an aura of tranquility, their graceful curves inviting peaceful repose.

Perfect place for an ambush.

"Captain." The dramatic soprano shattered the illusion of solitude.

Mon wheeled towards the sound, hands half-raised to defend herself, every muscle tensing before her brain could override the well-trained response.

And then override the jolt of distrust and fear.

Aimee Five glided into view from the opposite corner, a human-shaped synth, at least from the shoulders up. Her shimmer-silk head wrap and wide-skirted gown of vivid crimson were perfectly set against the bronze of her skin and the bed of shoulder-high corn behind her. Her elegance was meant to unsettle, Mon knew from experience. All crisp, porcelain lines and fluid movements.

Of course, she did have fancy wheels under that skirt for feet. But it wasn't just her body's composition that contributed to the perfection. Aimee Five was a well-practiced politician, having led the planet's High Council for five eventful years.

"Station Chief." Mon willed her shoulders to relax into a casual slouch, aiming for nonchalance. Trying not to let the synth know how much her presence raked claws of disquiet down Mon's spine, even as her logical mind tried to tamp down her body's ingrained fear of synths. "I'm surprised you called."

Aimee Five's full lips curved in a shadow smile. Her copper eyes, wide in their bronze human shape of a face, sparkled.

"Have a seat."

Mon settled gingerly on one end of the curved bench where Aimee Five had sat during the negotiations. Where Aimee Five's colleague, Allen, had sat. Where Mon's ward, Heather, had begged to stay here on Arkhide.

Aimee Five propped her butt on the garden bench, nowhere

near its woven-bamboo back. Her cool gaze roved over the lush garden surroundings.

Mon followed her line of sight. In the warm sun, the swaying bamboo had an almost hypnotic quality. All of it, such a sense of abundance, such a thrum of life.

A weighted pause hung between them as Mon grappled with her unease. Synthetic humans, with their artificial near-perfection and their enigmatic ways, creeped her out. Augmented humans were shocking, but full synths? They were the stuff of nightmares, the villains in every space opera she'd ever seen.

But despite the sheer alienness of Aimee Five—and despite that Little Miss Society voice inside Mon's head screaming "Abomination!"—Mon had felt a begrudging respect for her from the first. It wasn't just the woman's sense of resilience, or her unruffled self-possession.

Aimee Five had led the government that sent the negotiator who bested the Cooperative on its own terms. Aimee Five herself, not even raising her voice, had talked down an infuriated diplomat during a murder investigation.

Mon had been sitting right next to the diplomat, watching it happen.

"Captain," Aimee Five said. "We have a problem."

Mon's chest went tight, a flicker of apprehension. She had hoped to speak with Heather first. Find out what was up, before facing the authorities. But the girl was on off-comms, apparently helping out in some emergency.

"Is it Heather?" Mon asked, her voice carefully neutral. "I know she can be a handful."

To Mon's surprise, Aimee Five shook her head, her expression softening.

"Not at all. Heather is doing remarkably well. Her insights and innovations—and her energy, oh my—have made her many friends here. We're thrilled to have her as part of our community."

Relief washed over Mon, as if a heavy air tank had lifted from her shoulders. One less damsel to save.

But if she wasn't here for Heather, what was she here for?

Obviously reading the unspoken question in her expression, Aimee Five leaned forward, her gaze intent.

"Actually, Mondrian Delacroix, it's you I wanted to discuss."

Chapter Two

Mon glanced away from Aimee Five, from that copper-plated X-ray gaze of hers. She inhaled the sweet scents of the orbital station's garden. The mint under the bamboo forest, the mist on leaves.

What could the Arkhideans possibly want from her?

She racked her brain. Had she made some big mistake the last time she was here? Did she owe them money?

"Sure you've got the right Listener?" she said, half-jokingly.

Aimee Five shifted forward again, toward Mon, fixing her with a stare that felt like a cortical scan. "Personally, no, I am not. But I was overruled."

The synth leaned back, glancing up and out, toward the windows. Toward Arkhide, her planet. That blue-white ball with the many brown spots of tiny islands and the many, many red spots of mighty volcanoes.

A very young, very seismically active planet, Arkhide should have been terraformed well before the migrants from the planet

Wala settled permanently on it. But when Wala was destroyed in a hideous accident not even two generations ago, these pioneer Arkhideans were all that remained.

"Allen talked me into it," Aimee Five continued, the hard brass of her voice softening. Her longtime advisor was the nicest, smilingest synthetic human Mon had ever met. "And your Heather."

"Heather?" Mon said. She wasn't following.

"Fine. Let me make it plain. We have a slight… issue on Arkhide. One that we think a Listener might be able to help us with. Problem is." She speared Mon with another one of those bone-scan glances. "It isn't something we want your Cooperative Realm to know about. Ever."

The buzzing in her head must be insects near. But Mon didn't dare break Aimee Five's eye contact.

"You're not tracking," Mon said. "You've already decided I'm not trustworthy. Obviously. I'm Cooperative. Central Command, even."

But Aimee was already speaking again in that rich, melodic soprano.

"Allen says, and Heather agrees, that you are no longer 3-C, if you ever were. You took the Cooperative's coin because there was a war on and they offered good training cheap. Once they had a bead on you, they left you alone to spy and run solo missions, and you let them paint you as a rebel and a chaos agent. Great cover story. Fooled me, for a while."

"Now the war's over," she continued, "and you're already hiding things from the Co-op. Entire people, in fact."

Mon pushed to her feet despite the tell it would be to the synth.

She couldn't sit still with her life all spread out like that. She thought all those details—especially the clandestine parts—were deep off the grid.

Evidently not.

"How do you know all this?"

"We do our research, too," Aimee Five said. "Plus, your Heather has the instincts of a fabulous spy. Too bad she can't keep her mouth shut."

She wasn't wrong about that. But still, it didn't add up.

"So you don't want Heather, because she'll talk. But why me?" Mon's voice matched the disbelief in her mind. "Surely there must be other Listeners out there, others who could help you." Although Co-op Central did try to scoop them up, all the ones they could find.

All the ones Mon had helped them find.

But she was done with that.

Aimee Five shook her head, her expression grim.

"Don't think we didn't look," she said. "Heather put the basic Listeners' test recordings on Arkhide's chat boards, and everyone who thought they might be one took the test. Not one passed. No one came close. Listeners are one in tens of millions; we are only tens of thousands."

For the first time since Mon had stepped into the garden clearing, Aimee Five's perfect composure fractured just a bit.

That didn't comfort Mon. She paced away from the synth, towards the tall, golden-tasseled corn stalks. The whirr of the wind through the tassels crowded her ears.

So they knew all about her, and they didn't trust her. Why should she care? What stake did she have in the synths' problems?

"I don't need a job," Mon said.

"You're going to walk away from a real problem?" Aimee Five said. She sighed theatrically. "So unlike you."

"Not my problem," Mon said. Facing away this time, she knew the synth couldn't read her face. Luckily, because she was starting to waver.

Aimee Five sighed. "It's such a puzzle," she said. "Nobody's been able to crack it."

Dead hit. Mon never could turn down a puzzle. And an Arkhidean-proof puzzle? Safra's tits, just the thought made had her salivating.

But a puzzle could come in a message packet. It didn't need face-to-face.

"Fine," she said, pacing back to stand in front of Aimee Five. "So you've done your homework on me. So you know I can keep my mouth shut. That's not the problem. So what is it?"

Aimee Five touched her chest, where a human's heart would be.

"May I have your word that, even if you don't help us, you will not tell your former masters about us?"

She had no idea.

Mon was done with the Cooperative Realm. They'd forced her to recruit—to steal—Listeners from every edge of the system. She'd served her time; she'd paid her debts. She wasn't giving them a single thing more. Ever.

Mon stopped directly in front of Aimee Five. She loomed over the seated synth.

"Yes."

Aimee Five smiled, slow. She patted the bench where Mon had been sitting. Taking the power back.

Mon sat. It would be rude not to. But she slouched, resting her shoulders on the high back of the woven bench. She jammed her hands into the side pockets of her enviro-suit. This was the second time she'd come to a negotiation underdressed.

"On Arkhide, we have a base that's underwater," Aimee Five said.

"What?" Mon said. "I thought you-all avoided the water. And all this time you had an entire secret base?"

"We use it for... research."

That didn't sound sinister or anything.

And what about when that Co-op science sphere fell into the sea, and everyone on Arkhide nearly had a heart attack trying to get it out? Then again, the sphere had arrived without warning, and nobody knew it didn't mean harm.

"The base is for research, as I said. And protection." Aimee Five waved a perfectly tapered hand toward the planet. "We need to monitor seismic activity, constantly. The spot where the base is located gives particularly strong—and accurate—warning of impending trouble."

"Volcanoes?"

"And earthquakes, and tsunamis. The base can usually give us two-days' warning. Sometimes even three. With two days' advance notice, we can move an entire city and all its peoples from an endangered island to a safer one. That's where your Heather is now, helping with a migration."

That sounded just plain impossible. Mon couldn't stop to ponder that.

She glanced away from Aimee Five, her mind running down the implications. That couldn't be all the base was doing. There must be something else.

Something the Cooperative would be more interested in than weather emergencies.

She glanced back and met Aimee Five's gaze, her eyes narrowed.

"Okay, great. I'll keep your secret. So spill."

Aimee Five's expression grew severe.

"I'm telling you this because the majority of the people of Arkhide voted in favor of it. I did not."

Wow, so the entire planet knew all of Mon's business. Fantastic.

"The base has been been picking up strange signals," Aimee Five said. "Signals that we can't decipher—and not for want of trying."

Mon sat up straight.

"Signals?" she said. "Like you've never heard before?"

"Or seen," Aimee Five said. "If it's communication, part of it is outside our perception. It must be. And we've tried all manner of scans." For the first time, frustration flattened her perfect bell of a voice. She took a breath.

"Your talents, Mondrian Delacroix, extend far beyond the mere scope of your Listener abilities," she said. "Your exploits during the war and after show you possess a preternatural intuition, an ability to perceive patterns and possibilities that even our most advanced intelligences cannot replicate. Your mind is not bound by rigid constraints of programming or logic. It flows, like the tides of a thousand oceans."

Yeah, so that was coming on strong. Despite herself, despite the lingering wariness pulsing through her mind, Mon felt a reluctant flush of heat rising up her nape. Was that admiration she detected in Aimee Five's voice? Maybe, even, a hint of envy?

"You want me to go to an underwater research base, your only one," Mon said. "To Listen. Try to understand. That's it?"

"It's not a simple assignment," Aimee Five said. "I suggested we tap Heather. She said she is up for it."

She would.

"You are absolutely not sending a seventeen-year-old down into some dank base underwater all by herself."

Aimee Five mock-groaned. "Not you, too. I got an earful of

that from Allen." She flicked a hand, as if batting the idea away. "No, we are not. We're asking you."

Only now did Mon remember to negotiate. When the hook was sunk deep. She'd have to get better at this now that she was in the real world.

"What's in it for me?" she said, knowing how weak her position was. "Room and board and no glory?"

Aimee Five threw back her head and laughed at that, the unexpected peal of amusement filling the garden clearing with silvery, sparkling mirth.

"Pretty much. No, listen. This data contains mysteries and, I expect, revelations that could shatter our current understanding of the very nature of this universe and our place within it. The scientists and analysts may be stymied, but you... you might unravel those knots, Mondrian Delacroix. Not as some glorified operative or spy, but as an autonomous explorer sailing uncharted seas of pure potentiality."

Mon blinked, caught off-guard by the sheer audacity of Aimee Five's proclamation. It struck chords of yearning and skepticism in equal measure, notes of both temptation and caution.

She found herself leaning forward despite her lingering reservations, drawn in by the synthetic woman's sheer gravitational charisma and conviction.

Scanning for any sign of Mon's true feelings on her face, Aimee Five's expression sobered, the humor draining away like a receding tide, replaced by something fierce.

Slowly, unconsciously, Mon found herself nodding in mute acknowledgment of the possibilities unfurling before her. A sly, feral grin curved her lips as she held Aimee Five's copper stare with her own liquid brown gaze.

The synthetic woman's perfect features remained impassive,

though Mon didn't miss the answering glint of approval, of reciprocated ferocity, in her gaze.

Aimee Five rose from the bench in one sinuous motion, extending an elegant hand out towards Mon in silent invitation.

Steeling herself, Mon reached out and clasped the proffered hand. Aimee Five's cool fingers offered a startling contrast to Mon's own overheated palm.

"Follow me," Aimee Five said.

Chapter Three

Lumbering down the last few of the five hundred steps to Arkhide's Base Six, Mon felt the weight of the ocean pressing in. Her lungs weren't sure about the new mix of air needed here at one hundred meters below. Her limbs weren't sure they could hold her up.

Oh, to be twenty again.

The cool, damp air carried a faint scent of salt and metal. The rough-hewn gray stone walls of the stairwell softly echoed the tromp of her footsteps and nothing else, creating an eerie sense of isolation. Well, except for the ever-present happy hums of the power conduits and air pipes and comms relays flowing along the walls and ceiling.

At the bottom of the stair, she found a well-lit flat area big enough for two square metal cargo elevators to sit a ways away from each side of the stair. The elevators must go right inside the domed sandcrete storage shed she'd seen up-top attached to the stairwell entrance.

Would've been nice to know about that.

Mon stepped onto the stone landing but didn't move toward the wide brushed-metal airlock door ahead of her. Instead, she sat down on the last step with a huff.

Should have packed some water.

Soon there would be two domed storage sheds up-top. The beater courier ship she'd "borrowed" from the Co-op to come here (to pick up more headsets, officially) shouldn't have been able to drop into Arkhide's atmosphere, much less land on this little spit of an island. But the synths had installed one of their snazzy force-field boxes, which wrapped the whole ship safely while keeping the flight controls soft and responsive. She hadn't even felt the heat rise as she hit stratosphere.

The wires holding the elevator to her left started to grind and hum. Must be her baggage, coming down. The four robots—synths, she thought, but not human-form—that had been waiting for her up-top were efficient. They and their sandcrete extruder had laid half the circular foundation for the dome that would hide her ship before she'd finished her post-flight checks. One had told her to leave her baggage and pointed to the door to the stairs.

They might've mentioned the elevators.

Mon pushed herself up and dragged her feet toward the noisier elevator. Just as she saw its double-wide doors slide open, she heard the airlock behind her unseal.

The human-shaped synth—well, except for the extra set of arms near their waist—radiated an aura of energy that seemed to defy the crushing pressure of the ocean depths. Even their short brown buzz cut seemed to sparkle. Their sturdy golden-hued frame was clad in the ever-practical khaki coveralls techs all over the system seemed to favor. The many many pockets at hips, knees, everywhere else were filled with an assortment of things. More tools hung from a belt that looked made of woven seagrass.

"Hello! I'm Aster, your friendly neighborhood base manager

and tour guide!" Their warm voice echoed off the natural rock formations. "Welcome, Captain Delacroix, to our little corner of the deep blue-green."

Mon couldn't help but return the smile. Quite the change from the "Leave it" and "Over there" she'd heard from the synth upstairs. Aster must have voted on the chat boards in favor of letting her in.

"Mon is fine," she said.

"I see they gave you a good rebreather," Aster said, peering around Mon's shoulder to look at the backpack-style mini air tank and equipment on top of her duffle. "You'll want to keep that with you at all times. On your back, in fact."

Mon put it on and adjusted the straps. It was as heavy as it looked. But that meant it wasn't, really. Everything felt heavier down here.

"We've never needed to use the tanks, but it pays to be safe." They chuckled. "Plus it makes you all look like turtles, which is never not funny." They picked up her duffel as if it didn't weigh anything.

As they stepped into and out of the standard airlock, and walked down a standard main corridor, blue-light bars along its sides, Mon felt right at home. She could be on one of the Co-op's transports, for all the difference she saw.

Aster led her past various doors and airlocks, pointing out the bunk rooms, exercise areas, living spaces, and then the kitchen and dining area, a cozy space nestled between the living quarters and the power station.

The warm light from the overhead fixtures cast a welcoming glow on the standard appliances and the four small round tables with those armless chairs that were never quite comfortable. At least these were red and green, not the usual tan.

The aroma of fresh brewed coffee mingled with the ever-present scent of salt, a familiar blend that reminded Mon of long nights spent working on her ship.

The most striking difference was the outer wall of the area. Exposed stone, white with warm golden veins in the yellow-hued light.

They were in the ground. Under ground.

Deep under ground.

Exiting into water. High-pressure water.

They couldn't just run up the stairs to get away. They had to come up slow, to avoid the bends.

Which was just fine.

Mon let her mental Listener blocks down. Immediately, her mind was flooded: ten different hums of the various life support systems. Thousands of plink-pocks of circuits switching. Loud, the nearby gurgle of water through the pipes. All familiar, all well.

Aster gestured for Mon to take a seat at the nearest table, its metallic surface cool though the room was warm, and then stepped toward the kitchen counters.

"You look beat. Coffee?"

Mon waved her hand no. This wasn't the kind of tired coffee could fix.

"Didn't tell you about the elevators, did they?" Aster chuckled as they picked up a familiar-looking box from the counter and brought it to the table. They sat across from her. "I'll give you the short version and then let you take a rest."

The box was the kind Heather used to pack her headsets.

"Your friend sent you some stuff you'll need," Aster said. "Good things, friends." They didn't hand the box to her, but held it between their top hands.

"Anyway, first thing is, we don't really have days here. We're on the edge of twilight, sun-wise. So we follow our own rhythms, and the lights follow us. When you wake, your room lights will be the brightest they will be all day. When you return, they'll be the dimmest."

"So people don't spend a lot of time in their rooms," Mon said. "Good to know."

"Most folks spend their days at their station, in the kitchen, in the workout room, or in one of the two recreation areas. One room is for doing quiet things; that one has the ocean view. The other— the one I pointed out—is for doing boisterous things. That one has the big sound system and equally big dampening cushions on the walls."

"How much time do you spend outside?"

"After the first month, not much. Mostly you collect specimens —data—that you spend the next few months studying." Aster shrugged. "If that's what you're doing. Other folks here are doing simple mining and cargo collecting, which we use servos for."

"Is everyone here... enhanced?"

Aster looked at her as if she'd asked whether gravity worked.

"Right," they said. "Onto the gifts." They pushed the box toward Mon.

Inside was a beautiful fuzzy sky blue sweater, folded tightly to fit into the dinner-plate-sized box. Mon pulled it out reverently. A small, tied fabric bag slipped out of its folds. Aster caught before it hit the table.

The sweater had long sleeves, cork buttons, two side pockets, and the most beautiful textured weave. Like braided grass, from shoulder to hem. There was a note in one of the pockets.

"Mon! We need to talk. So put this on, and the headset, too."

Heather. Mothering her. Mon shook her head.

Aster had the small bag opened. They poured the contents into their hand. A fussy style of wristcom and a clear bag containing what looked like fake scar tattoos.

"To get you fully integrated into life down here, you'll need this," Aster said, opening the clear bag and poking a finger in. "These are divers' headsets. Heather modified them to work for Listeners like you." They pulled out their finger. One of the tattoos had stuck to it. "May I touch you?"

Mon nodded.

"Turn your head so I can reach one of your ears." She did so. Aster pulled on the tattoo; it stretched three times longer, into more of a line than a scar. They tapped one sticky end behind her ear, and then stretched the rest down and over the back of her jaw.

"This headset will allow you to tap into the base's communication network and access the various networks." They handed her the wristcom. She made the handshake to dupe her current comm's data to the new one. She had to put the new one on to complete the ID check.

"Give it a moment," Aster said, "to calibrate and sync up."

Mon closed her eyes, taking a deep breath as she felt the headset come to life. Suddenly, a rush of sensations flooded her mind—a cacophony of voices, images, and data streams. She gasped and grabbed the edge of the table.

She slammed all her Listener walls down. The chaos remained.

"Whoa there!" Aster said. Their hands gripped Mon's shoulders across the table, keeping her vertical. "Take a breath. I heard it could be a bit much at first. But you'll get used to it. Everybody does," they said with a slight lift at the end, as if they weren't exactly sure about that.

Mon nodded, her jaw spasming as she fought to regain control over the onslaught of information crowding her thoughts. Slowly, the chaos began to subside, and she found herself able to navigate the various channels and data streams—and find the blasted shut-offs. She sighed in relief.

"Maybe should start with channels off," she said.

"Heather said you'd say that," Aster said, humor lacing their words. "But she figured if she did that, you'd never turn them on, and she wanted to make sure you saw everything."

Blasted girl. But she was right. The WorldNet stretched out before her, a vast, interconnected web of knowledge and communication that spanned the globe and didn't stop there. Voicechat groups and boards buzzed with activity; she was sure the text and visual nets that she could pull up on the wristcom's screens would be faster than her unaugmented eyes could track.

How did this thing even work?

As she explored further, a blinking notification caught her eye —a message from Heather, waiting in her local inbox. Mon's heart leaped at the sight of the girl's name, but the headset's overwhelm made it difficult to focus on a single message. She'd read it later.

"Right," Mon said, her voice tight as she mentally hit mute on the last feed. "Might take a bit to get used to."

Aster pinged her, the softest tap right behind her ear. At her startled glance at them, they winked.

"Wait till you've got the hang of it. You'll never want to give it up."

As they walked back toward the exit stairs, Aster took Mon's hand. She hadn't realized how visibly wobbly she was.

Great.

Aster set the duffel against the inside wall of Mon's nook of a bedroom. A narrow bed, its head against the cave wall, and a new-smelling pressed-wood standing cupboard for her clothes occupied the space. A combo pressed-wood desk/table/workspace with a good light above and a portable standing lamp to the side. Across from that, a recliner made of some tufted fabric that looked incredibly welcoming.

Definitely not a room on a spacer ship.

Aster handed Mon a carton of juice and a couple of NutriBars they must have cadged from the kitchen.

"NutriBars! Trust me, they're the height of underwater cuisine." They rolled their eyes. "Water and glasses in the shared bathroom, there."

Mon managed a grateful smile. Her body felt like sand; her mind like pulled taffy. What time was it? Hadn't it been morning when she arrived? She had no idea.

"Thanks, Aster. I really appreciate it."

"No worries. Everybody feels this way, the first day." They glanced off to the side, down the hall toward the water. "We'll meet Olve tomorrow." They almost winced. "When he'll feel a little friendlier. We hope."

No news there.

"I've heard he can be a bit intense."

Aster nodded, their golden-brown skin glinting in the warm light. "That's one word for it. Asshole is another. Brilliant, driven, and utterly focused on his work." They patted Mon's shoulder. "But you, I think, are going to be a surprise."

"And I, for one, am looking forward to it," they said, smiling as they stepped back and let her room's door slide shut.

That didn't sound ominous or anything.

Mon sipped the juice.

So. Here she was, at the bottom of the sea, on a non-Cooperative Realm planet. Not really following the post-military life plan, now was it?

Ha. What plan?

She'd been single-mindedly focused on counting down the days to mustering out. Getting out. Busting out.

But getting into something else? She'd kind of forgotten that part.

Her immediate plan had been to settle in some quiet resort town, one with a good PTSD counselor, and a lot of down time.

Well, she'd tried that. And lasted two months.

She'd actually contemplated heading home. Meaning, wherever her foster parents happened to be. Both xenoarcheologists, they had been raving lately about what they were finding at a new site out in the spiral drift. They always had a bed for her, and hugs. And a trowel.

And the visit would kill another two months, tops.

Mon was actually kind of glad Aimee Five had called, except for all the worry over Heather. It postponed the decision yet again.

Surely, all she needed to decide on how to spend the rest of her life was a couple of months of really distracting activity.

The NutriBar was as chewy bland as ever. Mon set it aside after one bite and lay on her bed. She opened her senses to the comforting whirrs and rumbles and roars of a working facility.

She'd worry about it tomorrow.

Chapter Four

Mon stepped through the doorway into the main research lab and let the door whoosh shut.

The long, tall rectangular room was a testament to meticulous organization. Every piece of technology and collection of research material was frighteningly precisely arranged.

No mess? It looked like no working lab she'd ever seen.

In front of her stood a veritable castle of a workstation. Jammed against the short inner wall and nearly shoulder height, the workstation's standard-gray surfaces and storage looked ready for even the harshest sergeant's inspection. The thing took up one-quarter of the room.

Floating data screens cast moving, multicolored patterns across its neat surfaces and perfectly tidy bookshelves. It didn't even smell funky or dusty. More like dried oregano. Whiteboards and clearboards filled most of the space within the castle's walls, easily reached by the single person in the castle's center.

To her left, past the narrow walk left by the workstation, the long inner wall carried floor to ceiling glassy shelves. Specimens, all neatly labeled. Plant and rock samples or ancient-looking crockery basked in the soft glow of ribbon lights directly above.

On the matte-dark floor in front of the shelves, a shiny oval conference-style table looked large enough for a dozen people, but currently offered only enough chairs to seat four. Past the table was the short outer wall with a doorway. Storage, maybe, since there couldn't be that much more space before you hit the cave wall.

And along the long outer wall stretched the dusky green ocean.

Mon drifted toward the series of tall windows, eyes only for this new world.

At two hundred meters below the surface, it was a twilight world. The sun's rays barely penetrated this far, casting a haunting green-blue hue over everything. The water seemed unnaturally still, only occasionally disturbed by slow-moving shadows. Faint biolu-minescent glows flickered here and there, like stars twinkling in an inverted evening sky. The only plant life was a slow rain of bits and pieces from above.

Two spotlights on either side of the windows cast luminous beams into the murk. Lumpy fish and thick eels would slide in and out of their funnels of light.

The scene outside was nearly silent, the thick water muting all but the most significant movements. Mon could almost taste the metallic tang of the seawater in the back of her throat, mingling with her breath. Almost feel the cold embrace of the deep through the reinforced glass, a stark reminder of the ocean's relentless pressure.

At the far end of the windows stood the tall clear cube of an airlock. Its inner door was steps away from the storage room; its outer door led to a wide metal-mesh deck. The deck stretched the length of the windows. You could put on a dive suit, step outside, and just sit and stare. In fact, two plastic deck chairs sat tucked away on one side.

That's what must be in that storage room—dive gear.

The air in this room was warm and dry, an odd contrast to the mildly humid chill of the corridor outside. A faint scent of ozone and plastic rose from the hard-working electronics and optical equipment. The soft hums of the room's equipment and its life systems couldn't fill the space, a background that emphasized the room's severe library atmosphere.

Looking out, Mon felt much sharper than yesterday. Amazing what a ten-hour sleep and surprisingly satisfying breakfast could do. The coffee, in particular, had been a revelation—rich, smooth, and invigorating, it had banished the lingering fog of exhaustion and disorientation that had clung to her since she got here. Must have some matcha or the local equivalent in it.

Which reminded her, eventually, that someone else was in the room.

Who must be Olve. His lean frame with its turtle backpack backup air supply sat hunched over two big screens in his castle of a workstation. His dark hair, streaked with gray at the temples, swept back from his face to his shoulders in a careless style that spoke of long hours spent running his fingers through it in concentration. His brow furrowed. His eyes, so pale they seemed to shift and change with the changing light from the screens, were locked onto the data flowing in front of him.

Mon took a step forward, scuffing her boots on purpose against the seamless, matte-black flooring. The sound, though slight, was enough to draw Olve's attention. He glanced up, his gaze flicking over Mon with a brief, assessing intensity before returning to his screens. A curt nod was his only acknowledgment.

Rude.

For a moment, she just stood there. Then she cleared her throat, the sound unnaturally loud.

"Hello," she began, her voice measured and professional, "I'm Mon Delacroix. Here to help you with your puzzle."

Olve's fingers paused on the screen, and he turned to face her fully. His expression was meant to be unreadable, a carefully constructed mask. But it was too stiff.

He was furious.

"I'm aware of who you are, Captain Delacroix," he said, voice clipped. "And yeah, no."

Mon let the flicker of irritation show on her face, but she kept her voice even.

"I didn't invite myself here. Your government sent me."

Olve's eyes narrowed, and he leaned back in his chair, his arms crossing over his chest in a gesture that seemed equal parts defensive and dismissive.

"Because of your 'unique skills?'" he said. "Captain. You are a Listener, a spy, a Cooperative Realm lackey. How exactly do you believe you can contribute to my research?"

Mon took a deep breath and held it until she had her voice under control. It only took a second.

"You're right," she said, voice firm but not challenging. "My background is unconventional for this kind of work."

Olve snorted.

"But my skills are undeniable. And you'd be a fool to pass up the chance to see if they can be useful. All ports in a storm, right?"

"It's any port in a storm," he said. "Fine. Here."

She felt a ping behind her ear. On her wristcom she saw hundreds of notices of files loading into some shared workspace she'd need a bigger screen to look at.

"Go catch up on the data," he said. He waved toward the pressed-board conference table on the other side of the room. Apparently there was no workstation for the intern.

Mon turned away from him in a perfect Cooperative Corps

pivot despite her body feeling as if it weighed twice as much, and didn't scowl until she was facing full away. At least the black padded chairs with arms looked comfortable. She dropped into one gratefully.

Earlier, she'd spent breakfast familiarizing herself with her new comms device. The initial overwhelming flood of information and sensory input had given way to a more manageable flow. Now, she felt easy pulling up two screens and opened the shared workspace.

As Mon settled into analysis mode, she let her Listener senses expand, reaching out to explore the intricate web of sounds, sensations, and subtle energies that permeated the base and the ocean beyond. The low, constant hum of the life support systems and the soft, rhythmic pulsing of the power conduits formed a soothing backdrop.

But beneath that comforting familiarity, she sensed other, odder currents. The faint, high-pitched keening of the water, moving against metal, and, lower-pitched, against rock. Some angry sounding water creature, its discordant tones fading as it moved farther from the base.

And something else, something deeper and more elusive—a pulsing, primal energy that seemed to emanate from under her feet. Was there another cave under this one?

With a mental shake, Mon turned her attention to the screens floating in front of her, her eyes scanning the dense matrices of data and analysis that Olve had dumped in a mess in her lap. Complex linguistic models, some scans that looked weirdly similar to anatomy drawings, reams of raw sensor data and environmental readings.

But it was all just data, familiar. Mon began to notice patterns and connections, and dove deeper.

Her train of thought was interrupted by the softest tap from behind her ear. New file. Brand new—Olve must have put her on the auto-forward list. A written report, a detailed accounting of the trade and resource exchanges between the base and its suppliers.

But this was no ordinary commerce. Seafloor sulfides, manganese, polymetallic nodules. Traded for a large amount of something called "green gel."

Why would Arkhideans need so much of any color gel down here? And who was finding these rare metals to exchange?

Everywhere she looked, another puzzle.

Everywhere, missing data. So much information, with all the important bits gaping holes.

Enough of this.

She pushed her chair back, ready to stomp on over to Olve, demanding answers and explanations. But before she could stand, the door to the lab slid open and Aster burst in, their face a mask of concern and agitation.

"Olve, Captain, I do apologize," they said, voice tight. "I meant to be here to introduce you, but I got caught up in a red-flag problem with the supply chain I had to handle immediately."

"Not those NutriBars, again?" Olve didn't even look up.

Aster didn't spare a glance for Olve as they made their way to Mon. They sat in the seat beside her, leaning forward.

"How's it going?" they said, soft.

Mon shrugged. "I'm reading in, no problem. But—" She widened the screen view of the trade report. "I thought this was a research lab. Who's doing all this trading?"

"Ah, yes," Aster said, leaning back. Louder, he said, "Well. I suppose it's about time we told you about all that."

"It is not," Olve snapped from his side of the room. "Send her back. She doesn't know anything. She doesn't need to know anything."

"Olve." Aster's voice pleading and resigned. They'd obviously talked about this to death.

Olve stood up, his eyes slits. "Don't tell her anything. Co-op spy."

That was enough asshole for one day.

Mon lurched to her own feet, ready to brawl.

"Enough!" she said. "I am not here as your enemy, Olve. Or your competition, whatever. I'm just here to solve the puzzle."

She took a breath. Aster nodded vigorously, their relief palpable.

Olve said nothing.

"You want the puzzle solved, right?" she said. Whatever the bleeding puzzle was. "Then you should accept help from all quarters."

"Not from the Cooperative," he sneered.

She was so done with him.

"She's right, Olve," said Aster, still trying hard. "We need all the help we can get, and Captain Delacroix—Mon—has skills that we don't. We can't keep pretending we can handle this on our own."

Olve's jaw clenched. He lifted his hand to slash it down, shutting off any further discussion.

But Mon wasn't paying attention anymore.

A haunting sound filled her mind. A shimmering vibrato shivered through her bones. Her head whipped around, her Listener senses straining to locate the source of the resonance before it flayed the last membranes of her nerves. It wasn't a bad feeling, really. Just too blasted loud.

It was coming from outside, from the left.

Coming closer.

She stepped closer to the window. She reached out to touch it, but stopped short. The absolute chill of the reinforced material radiated out, a reminder of the crushing pressure that lay just beyond.

Mon looked hard left. Nothing so far.

Something pinged on Olve's bank of screens.

"Blast it all," he said. "You heard that?"

Aster joined Mon at the window.

"How far out?" he said.

"Two minutes. Less."

The sound-sense was overwhelming. Mon felt Aster touch her shoulder. She was vibrating visibly. She calmed her breath and ran through all the blocking techniques she'd developed, one by one.

There, thinking about houses made of cotton, that quieted the sound down to conversation level.

She sighed. The dark of the ocean had lightened to an olive blue. Must be daytime up-top.

The sound altered, from sharp and grating to smooth.

Careful, somehow.

Masked.

A dark shape emerged from the shadowy waters below. A sinuous, undulating form, nothing like she'd ever seen.

Mon stiffened, military style.

Assess the threat.

The creature was massive, easily twice the size of a human, with a sleek, segmented body that shimmered and pulsed with bioluminescence, blue, green, purple. In front its two large multifaceted eyes glowed or swirled faintly in the sparse light from the base. Probably didn't like bright light.

It had at least ten tentacle-leg-arm-things, all on the underside. It swam closer to the window using the four back ones, its movements graceful and precise. When it reached a meter's distance away, it settled upright, its four thick tentacles drifting down.

Its back—exoskeleton—looked hard as diamonds. Better to go in through its underside, the softer-looking flesh between all the pairs of tentacles.

Mon stepped forward, transfixed by the creature's strangeness and the power of its song.

She wasn't afraid of big shrimps.

So long as they were on the other side of the window.

Olve joined them at the window. He lifted one hand, palm out, at the glass.

The creature lifted one of its thinner tentacles—arms—in the same fashion. The arm tapered into three long, thin appendages, luminescent dots lining their edges. It was swirls of colors, even at this dusky depth.

Then the creature started to move a pair of arms, in a regular pattern.

It was signing.

In Galactic Sign Language.

Sweet bloody Safra. A sentient species.

A secret sentient species.

Mon tried to keep up with the conversation, but her GSL was rusty and both Olve and the creature were fast. She thought she caught "why?" and "later."

"They want to know where the green gel is," Olve said flatly. "They expected it yesterday."

Aster sighed.

"That's what I was working on, this morning. Tell them, couple days. Three days, to be safe."

Even Mon could tell that was the wrong answer. The creature's signs grew more curt.

"Can we give them part?" Olve said.

"It's all made," Aster said. "No kegs is the problem."

In his response, Olve made the sign for fuel tank. Keg must not be an easy word to share.

The response surprised him. He nodded yes before seeming to remember that he needed to make the sign for yes.

The creature matched his nod. It turned its head toward the ocean. In a flash of waving glassy tendril-legs, it was gone.

Soon its original song exploded out again. Mon pressed her hand to her forehead, trying to stop the overwhelm. But it already was fading. The creature was heading straight away from them and down, fast.

"They're going to get some of the old kegs," Olve said. He turned to Aster. "Should've thought of that."

Mon blinked, shaking her head to clear the lingering fog of the creature's song. She stepped back to get both of them into her range of view.

"So," she said, her voice unsteady. "That's the secret."

Chapter Five

Mon sank to the floor, her legs giving way as the weight of the moment swamped her. She could not catch her breath. She'd seen strange and wondrous things in her travels across the system, but nothing like this.

The sheer enormity of it. She struggled to make sense of what she had seen. Had felt. Was feeling.

A sentient alien species.

Blasted freaking comets.

Beside her, Aster lowered themselves to the ground, matching her cross-legged position. Their multi-faceted eyes sparkled with excitement—or worry.

"Well, that was a thing," they said, their voice a forced light-hearted. "I guess you could say the Ren'kari really make a splash."

The joke fell flat.

Mon, dazed, still caught Olve's withering glare at Aster. Olve had not dropped to the floor. Instead, the researcher paced the room as if the ferocity of his strides would make it wider. She had no time for him.

Trying to focus on Aster, she kept seeing the creature. Ren'kari. All shiny eyes and exoskeleton and so many arms and legs. Tentacles.

The implications were enormous.

Social. Philosophical.

Political.

These guys were going to blow people's minds.

Aster touched her knee.

"Mon?"

"How long have you known about them?" she asked, her voice barely above a whisper.

Aster glanced at Olve before answering.

"We've always known about them. The first Walan explorers found them forty—fifty—years ago. In the core scans." The extensive series of deep-planet scans that helped the geoengineers plan for terraforming.

Terraforming.

"These guys... told you to leave their planet alone," Mon said. She looked out at the water again, seeing a ghost outline of the creature in the way the faded light moved through water.

"They're amphibious," Aster said.

Mon frowned. So?

"They ceded us the land, on the promise that we would do nothing harmful to the water. Throw nothing—no trash—into it. Travel in the agreed-upon lanes."

"We're tenants, here," Olve said from the other side of the room. He pivoted and started walking toward them again. "Not colonizers."

So that explained Arkhide's motto, Stewards of the Land. The phrase wasn't throwback to some imaginary idyllic past, it was the literal truth.

"You shouldn't have stayed here," she said. "It's their planet."

"What choice did we have?" Olve stomped a foot right next to her. "You blew up our home planet."

She refrained, barely, from elbowing him behind the knee.

Anyway, he did have a point.

Aster patted the air down, apparently trying to wave Olve into calm. Olve huffed and returned to pacing.

"In fact, yes, the plan was to keep moving," Aster said. "But the Ren'kari thought of something better. Mutual trade. They'd done it before."

"Who with?" This sector was sparse in terms of livable planets. Did these Ren'kari have space travel, too?

"See those artifacts?" They pointed at some of the glassware and other everyday objects on the shelves. "They're from the first human settlement. At least we think they were human. They knew some sign language, but not GSL."

"Idiots." Olve was stomping toward them again. "They made all the promises, but at some point broke them." Pivoting, he waved toward the window and the sea beyond. "Amphibious creatures can get to you on land, too."

"They came up in the night and wrecked the colony," Aster said. "We've found wreckage from two sites."

Mon looked toward the shelves with the artifacts.

"Could I look at them?"

"Please do," Olve said peevishly. "Let's everyone get off the floor, at least."

Behind the chair where she'd been sitting earlier, Mon found what looked like dinner plates and a cook pot. She picked up a plate, light green ceramic. The marking on the back looked like an artisan's mark, not a fabrication. Or maybe the fabricator was the artisan?

"How old is this?"

"That's the funny bit," Aster said. "Our scanners say round-about one thousand standard."

She tapped the plate with a fingernail. The tone it made was pure. It shouldn't even exist, anymore. Must have been buried, most of that time.

She scanned the other shelves. "Crockery. Woodwork. No tech."

Olve threw himself into the chair at the end of the table. It rocked dangerously but did not tip. Dust rose from it that smelled for all the world like cheese puffs.

"They said they threw it all—and the people—into a volcano," Olve said. "At least we think that's what they said." He ran both his hands through his hair, clasping them behind his neck in a way that looked painful.

"Their language is unlike anything we've encountered before," Aster said. "Sound, light, and chemical signals in an interplay that defies conventional analysis."

"I see." She set the plate back into its holder and turned back to the table. Another mystery for later. "But now they can sign. Some-what," she said just as Olve was about to interrupt. "And you are able to trade. Rare minerals for some kind of jelly?"

"Nutrient gel," Aster said. They seated themselves on Olve's right, across from Mon. "Important to the Ren'kari."

"To bad they don't like those NutriBars." Olve grimaced. Mon worried for his neck. He was young, but that position couldn't be good. "I'd be willing to give all those away," he said.

Aster shook their head, smiling. They patted Olve's elbow. The move seemed to unlock Olve's hands from behind his neck. Mon could see the deep bond between the two. Shared experiences, mutual respect.

"I've seen a lot of strange things in my time," Mon said, her tone softening. "But nothing quite like this. That creature—Ren'kari? Incredible."

Olve's face lit up with a genuine smile.

He was kind of cute, for a thirty-something obsessive asshole.

"I remember when I first heard about them," he said, leaning his head against the back of the padded chair, taking the weight off his poor neck. "My friend's mom was so mad that we'd swum out so far into the bay, she threatened that the Water People would come and take us away forever. Water People! We laughed. Thought she was telling stories. But then she showed us the vids."

He glanced at Mon. "She had to put in a special code to get to them. And, oh. That moment I saw them I knew I had to get down here. I had to."

His mouth slowly closed, his gaze obviously not in the present.

Aster had been inspecting his nails as Olve told the story. They must have heard it before.

"It was supposed to be a six-month rotation," Aster picked up the story. "Like all the rotations. Then it was a year. Then two. Then he became the mentor—"

"Ha!" Olve said, bitter.

"And now we'll never get him out of here."

Without warning, Olve's mouth turned down, casting him back into crank mode. He rolled up in the chair to slam both palms on the table.

"And now you'll tell your non-cooperative masters all about them."

Why shouldn't she?

"Why didn't you?"

Olve glowered. "Not their business."

Aster lifted a hand, asking mercy.

"In fact," they said, casting an annoyed look at Olve before focusing on Mon. "It is the Ren'kari themselves who asked us not to. They are not interested in other species—not even us. We're not friends, really. More like roommates who do reciprocal favors for each other."

Mon racked her memory. What had Aimee Five said? Volcanoes.

"They warn you of the volcanoes," she said. "So you have time to prepare."

Olve touched the side of his nose. In some cultures that meant yes.

"And what do they get from us?" he said. "Green gel. That's actually white, or clear."

Mon shook her head. Another unbelievable detail in an unbelievable story.

Except it was true.

She gripped the edge of the table. How could the furniture in this room still be cool when her mind—her whole body—was on fire? She felt like she'd lived a whole day in the last half-hour.

But now she had another question. Roommates tried not to bug each other. Why send another human down to get in their business?

"So," she said. "Why are we bothering them?"

Olve's head snapped toward her, his gaze fire. "Pardon?"

"They're not interested in humans. The trade deal seems solid. Nothing's really wrong." She held her hands out, shrugging. "So why am I here?"

Olve shot to his feet, his eyes daggers.

Now what was up his ass?

Mon kept on. "Is it just, 'the more we know, the better neighbors we can be?'"

"Get out!" Olve's face pinched in as if her words had soured on his tongue.

What the hell?

Aster jumped up. "Wait!" They put a hand on Olve's shoulder.

"It's like this," they rushed to explain. "We often misunderstand each other and end up miscommunicating. Olve here estimates we're getting maybe twenty percent of what they're saying to us. We recently made a mistake—insulted one of them or something. We don't even know! But one of the Ren'kari ambassadors said they were reconsidering their agreement with us. With humans."

Mon gasped. Her hand went to her throat.

"They would kick you off the planet?"

Olve growled. "Did it before, didn't they?" He shook Aster's hand off his shoulder.

"There," he said. "That's the story."

He balled his hands into fists. "Take it back to your precious Cooperative Realm. Tell them all they have to do is wait, and soon the evil augments and synths will be homeless. Ripe for slaughter."

Bloody hell.

For the second time in an hour, Mon was so blindsided she couldn't come up with the proper epithet. More important, though, was to put out the fire. The flaming-red-faced man who looked like he was about to punch everything in sight.

"Stop," she said, soft. She lifted a hand, palm forward. She did not get out of her chair, despite all the muscles in her legs telling her to kick and run.

"I am not interested in seeing anyone get booted off their planet," she said. "I am especially not interested in seeing one more person get killed. My war's over."

Olve's strained breathing started to ease. His color stopped rising.

Aster moved to the other side of their friend, blocking Olve's access to Mon.

Mon lowered her hand. She touched the fingertips to the table to ease their shaking.

"If the Ren'kari don't want to talk to the Co-op, I'm not going to go against their wishes," she said. "We respect all peoples, as it says in our Universal Declaration of Rights."

She lifted her hand, palm up. Stretched it out, toward Olve.

"Let's solve this problem. Together."

Chapter Six

Mon woke with a start, her mind overflowing with the haunting, discordant harmonies of the Ren'kari. More than one, this time. An orchestral cacophony of vibrations resonated along her nerves and in her bones.

She sat up, rubbing her temples.

Too much.

She scrambled to grab her noise-canceling headphones from the bedside table, desperate to block out something. Lose the usual sounds so she could focus on building the walls to block to the alien sounds.

Now, before they overwhelmed her Listener senses and knocked her out.

As she slipped the headphones over her ears, the normal world fell away, leaving only the new world of the Ren'kari. Mon took a shallow breaths and focused her mind on the techniques that had worked yesterday.

Yesterday's block only handled one set of shrieks and discordant harmonies. Yesterday's visitor. Today, there were more.

Slowly, doggedly, she built mental walls against the others. Any single way—wrapping the feelings in cotton houses, making the sound into ice and shattering it, picturing an actual wall—didn't work, but piling them up seemed to do the trick.

Finally, she had at least a little space for her own thoughts.

She was going to have to get a lot better at this. And fast.

Mon glanced at the clock on her wristcom, its soft blue glow illuminating the dimly lit room. It was early, far too early for anyone else to be up and about. She swung her legs over the side of the bed, the cold stone floor sending a shiver up her spine, and grabbed her sweatpants and fuzzy socks. The soft, cozy material of the sweater Heather had given her felt like a comforting hug as she wrapped it around herself.

She got the stretchy-scar headset in place behind her ear and onto her jaw as she ran toward the lab. She was here to help Olve, and there he was, alone with all this noise. Why hadn't they called her?

They probably did call her, but her headset was off. Nobody here probably even thought to use the wristcom's alarms.

The sounds of the Ren'kari kept pushing on her mental walls. She had to get this under control. Outside her head, her heavy footsteps were the only sound in the empty corridor.

She should try fiddling with the controls on her headphones. Later.

The lab was brightly lit as she entered, and warm, but empty. Nobody in the water outside the window; nobody here in the room.

Then she heard a soft rumble.

Inside Olve's castle of screens and equipment, half underneath a shelf holding a sample fabricator, snored Olve. Blanket under his head, with another blanket over his body. Still wearing the turtle air-tank backpack. His head was tucked into the shadow of the desk. A thick sweep of hair had slid across his face.

Mon hesitated. Should she wake him? He'd obviously done this before, to have two blankets at the ready.

She backed out of the lab, careful not to make any more noise, and tapped her wristcom to ping Aster. When Aster's voice spoke directly into her right ear, even under her noise-canceling phones, she jumped. This sticky little comms link took some getting used to.

"He better be asleep," Aster said. They were somewhere with a lot of noise and voices in the background. "He was up all night waiting for the Ren'kari to bring the kegs. The rest of us are here in the cargo cave, filling them up quick as we can."

Mon scanned the hall. During their brief tour of the facility, Aster hadn't shown her how to get to any cargo cave. She didn't see any obvious stairs or door.

"How do I get there? I can help."

"Nah," Aster said. "We've got a rhythm going. We're good. But thanks for offering."

At least these links still made the familiar click when the call ended. Mon sighed out loud.

She made her way back to her room, changing into the pale yellow coveralls that Heather said flattered her raw sienna skin. She put the sweater back on and grabbed her extra pillow. As she passed the kitchen, she snagged a mug of coffee—with a lid, so hopefully Olve wouldn't smell it in his sleep, and two NutriBars. Too early to cook, or even heat anything up.

Back in the lab, Mon settled herself on the pillow next to the large observation windows. Sitting in chairs too long made her feet swell, and that was before you added in the pressure of the deep ocean bearing down on them. Not to mention the creaks in her nearly forty-year-old knees.

She pulled up two floating data screens, muting all the audios. On one screen, she composed a quick message to Heather, thanking her for the sweater and asking to borrow one of her souped-up Listener recording devices. If there was anything already built that could sense these Ren'kari signals, she'd put her money on Heather's gear.

On the other screen, she called up a video refresher course on Galactic Sign Language. She'd taken a summer intensive class in GSL, and tested proficient, but that was twenty years ago. Now she was only sure of the ones people used when working in the atmo-suits when the voice comms went out: this way, there, here, no, yes, go go go!

GSL was a pretty intuitive language—if Galactic was your native language. It wasn't hers, but as she mirrored the motions on the screen, the shape of the syntax came rolling back into her memory.

Not long after she started practicing, Mon felt as if she was being watched.

Couldn't be Olve, still breathing heavy there under his table.

A presence hovered at the edge of her peripheral vision, and at the edge of her consciousness. An active shift in the vibrations and harmonies that surrounded her.

A shadow on her screen.

With tentacles.

Mon froze.

But littler tentacles.

Mon thawed, and kept her eyes focused on the screen. Pretending not to notice the figure that hovered a meter or so from the window. Ren'kari, she was certain, but far less imposing than the one she'd seen yesterday. Maybe a child, curious about the strange human with the wildly swinging arms?

Her breath caught. Here was a chance to make contact outside formal channels. If the Ren'kari elders were indeed mad at the humans, maybe this little one could tell them why.

For a moment, she considered waking Olve.

Nah, let him sleep. If this kid could learn enough GSL in one session to express complicated thoughts, she'd eat a whole box of those horrid NutriBars. Wake Olve up when it was really time to talk.

Mon switched the GSL tutorial to the first lesson, basic greetings. She switched the interface from "GSL for Galactic speakers" to "GSL for non-Galactic speakers." In place of the written text the tutorial now showed pictures. Of course they were all of humans on land, but you couldn't have everything.

She did not look around. She did not act as if she'd seen anything behind her at all.

It was killing her.

The little Ren'kari drew closer, their shadow widening to touch her shoulder. In the window's reflection, their exoskeleton and limbs flickered with light.

To her Listener senses, the Ren'kari was a loose braid of interlocking vibrations. Sometimes the pulses seemed to match their body's changes in luminescence. Sometimes they seemed to argue with the shifting pattern of lights.

As Mon not-watched, the shadow of a Ren'kari tentacle—arm—began to mimic her movements, mirroring the video's movements. At first it was tentative, hesitant. But with repetition, the moves grew more assured.

Mon pushed repeat on the lesson.

When they'd covered "hello, hi, yes, no, goodbye" twice through, she dared a glance over her shoulder.

This Ren'kari seemed to have a less-developed exoskeleton than the other, more gray and less crystalline. Their sinuous front limbs tapered to the same three-pronged points, with delicate, almost crystalline structures at the tips. One arm was wrapped around something small and curved at the top of the window—a hand-hold? This Ren'kari needed an anchor?

But it was the Ren'kari's bioluminescence that grabbed her attention. Patterns of light flowed across their shell and down their limbs like living art, their swirls and shifts in color mesmerizing.

Blues and greens predominated, shot through with flashes of violet and gold that pulsed in time with something. The alien's movements? Their thoughts? Something else?

Suddenly, the small Ren'kari locked eyes with Mon. Their bioluminescent patterns flashed, a startled burst of red and purple.

In an instant, it darted away, vanishing into the shadows above the window.

Her glance had taken too long.

Mon sucked in a breath. Had she frightened the little guy away for good?

No, or not yet at least. That bit of an arm around the hand-hold was still there.

Mon shifted on the pillow, settling in a position she could hold still for as long as it took.

It took a count of forty.

Tentatively, the Ren'kari began to emerge. Just up to the bottom edge of its huge oval eyes, shiny bright swirls of gray and white. So tentative.

So curious.

Mon gave them a slow blink, the way she did with other people's pets.

It blinked back, slowly closing its side eyelids and then its vertical ones.

Sweet scents of dawn. They were communicating!

Mon stayed absolutely still. The kid slowly, hesitantly, pulled more of its body out of the shadow. Their arms were blinking wild colors and patterns, but their body had gone darker gray. Fear? Camouflage? She had so many questions.

Mon lifted her arm, close to her chest, slow, nonthreatening.

She gave the sign for "hello," holding her flat hand, palm facing out, in front of her chest and making the quietest little wave.

She did it again.

The Ren'kari paused, their lights dimming for a moment. Then, they raised one of their own limbs, the three narrow tips arranging themselves into a rough approximation of the sign.

Mon waved hello again.

The colors along the kid's carapace flashed on, dancing again.

They did their little wave again.

Mon shivered with delight. The pattern of lights on her new little friend's limbs seemed to mirror her emotion.

Her mind raced through the list of other basic signs. Which one to try next?

But before she could get her hands moving again, a sound like a massive bullfrog's croak shattered the moment. The young alien darted away, their bioluminescent patterns falling into deeper tones.

Mon jumped to her feet, and almost fell over. Stupid foot fell asleep.

The kid was already gone.

Blast it all to bits.

That spot behind her ear pinged. She accepted the call, and Aster's voice once again filled her right ear.

"You in the lab? Good. Wake up Olve. Shake him, it's okay. The Ren'kari ambassador is headed your way."

Chapter Seven

Surprising no one, Olve even woke up cranky.

But at least he woke up gears in motion.

He grabbed his coffee mug, saw it was empty, and ran out of the lab, barely waiting for the door to slide open. Mon watched him go. Her thermal mug was empty, and her legs still felt filled with heavy sand. A little more caffeine might not be bad.

But if the Ren'kari ambassador was as speedy as the little Ren'kari she'd just met, Olve wouldn't be back in time to greet them. Which left her. She sighed and scanned the lab, mentally running down the checklist of Big Meeting Prep she'd learned as a young cadet. She'd missed out on coffee back then, too.

The chairs were tucked in around the meeting table. No need to count them—or even to use them. Olve's workstation was the mildest mess, most of the mess well out of range of the window. No snacks needed. Everything in sight neat and tidy.

Except for her pillow, right in front of the main window.

Mon strode over to grab it. She picked it up with one hand and with the other swiped up the napkin next to it that had held the NutriBars. Those bars tasted like chewy socks. Rising, she tucked the napkin into her pocket.

Before she could turn to go put the pillow on a chair, another shadow fell over her.

The Ren'kari ambassador, just opposite her outside the window, settled their tentacles in the orderly way they had the day before. They weren't looking at her, exactly.

More like right through her.

Mon signed "hello" in GSL. The Ren'kari gave a curt "no" sign in response.

Okay, then.

Mon hugged the pillow to her chest, cataloging the differences between this Ren'kari and the smaller one she had just seen. This one had a more angular, sharply defined exoskeleton structure. It was transparent, not gray. Their movements seemed much more controlled. They did not need to anchor themselves by gripping a hand-hold. The shrieks she'd heard as it came closer to the base were gone. They were masking most of their song, again.

It was the same Ren'kari as yesterday.

Their bioluminescent patterns seemed more geometric and symmetrical. Maybe another instance of better control than the kid's? In addition to a thicker, harder exoskeleton, their main body carried what looked like silica-based ornaments shaped like spikes or blades. Jewelry? None were on their arms. She wasn't going to call them tentacles any more, not now that she'd seen how dextrous those fingers of theirs could be.

The spectrum of their luminescence was heavy on dark reds and purples, with orange. A bad mood?

So many guesses. So many ways to make a mistake.

Olve rushed back in, hair dampened and slicked back, two

thermal mugs in hand. He lifted one of the mugs toward Mon but then set it on the big meeting table. Rather an obvious move to get her away from the window, and the ambassador.

She didn't mind moved back to the big table, really. She was here to learn and assist, and back here she could observe objectively both sides of the conversation. Mon leaned against the edge of the table, dropping the pillow on Aster's chair. She tilted back the lid on the coffee and took a careful sip. Black, the way she liked it.

Olve, striding toward the window, downed a steaming-hot gulp of his coffee. Mon winced. If his was as hot as hers, he'd just seared the entire inside of his mouth.

Olve set the mug on the floor. So much for formality. Standing in front of the ambassador, he started with a slow bow. As he came up, he made the sign for hello and welcome.

The Ren'kari started gesturing with two of their arms, lights flashing all up and down their body.

Just moments into the conversation, Olve ran toward the airlock at the far end of the room, cursing. He passed its door to step into what must be the dive suit storage room and emerged with two bulky screens. Wrapped in thick, clear casings, the screens looked like a pair of Baby's First Tablets.

Olve opened the inner airlock door, set one tablet inside, closed the door, and pressed a button to fill the space with water. While the two doors were solid metal, the walls of the airlock were clear. Green-yellow water rushed into the space. It must be midday up-top.

Olve used thirty seconds it took to fill the airlock to rush back to his coffee and take another lava gulp. He pushed his hair out of his eyes again and tucked it behind an ear. He must season his coffee with cinnamon.

Outside, the Ren'kari had coasted over to the airlock. They

pressed a button to open the outer airlock door and reached in for the tablet. They returned to the middle of the central window to face Olve, carelessly leaving the door open.

The Ren'kari tapped on the screen with all three of the tips of one of its arms. Like a touch typist, fast and clean.

It didn't take long, but whatever it said made Olve gasp.

And then groan.

"Take this," he said, tossing her the tablet.

She had to grab for it before it hit the floor.

Olve started waving his hands in a very forceful style of GSL. Faster and faster. Madder and madder. His breaths grew more ragged with every exchange.

The Ren'kari's responses did not increase in speed. She caught "yesterday" and "no," and cursed her lack of memory for languages.

Mon gave up and looked at the tablet. Big chains of numbers, not all in the same kind of series. One looked like a velocity series. In the corner of the screen she saw a button that said, "Map it?"

Yes, please.

She pressed the button, and a multidimensional map appeared. Water, what must be islands, and something else. Big, messy, and, as the simulation started running, growing.

Flowing.

Volcano.

Shit.

This couldn't be the one Heather and the others were helping. No, this one looked to be in the future.

Not two days from now.

Outside, in the water a few meters behind the Ren'kari, kegs started floating up into view. Each barrel-shaped container—as big as a Ren'kari ambassador—was tied to another like a line of preschoolers.

A pulsing matte-black drone was at the head of the line. At the tail was the smaller Ren'kari, the one who had signed with her. Their colors looked better than when they'd scurried off; more bright hues and swirls.

The youngster did not look toward the window. They lingered with the kegs like they were all at the start of a parade, awaiting the signal to go.

Amid its languid responses to Olve's frantic gesturing—Mon thought she saw the sign for late, or later—the Ren'kari ambassador looked behind and noticed the kegs waiting.

They made another of those dinosaur-frog honks.

The smaller Ren'kari, colors vanishing, sped to the front of the parade. They did something to the drone, and the kegs started moving again, sinking below view.

Olve had said the Ren'kari preferred to live at around five hundred meters down. It was a concession on their part just to come up this high to talk with humans.

Olve cursed and stomped out of the lab.

What had happened?

The Ren'kari ambassador replaced the tablet in the airlock, closed the door, and pressed a button. She felt the airlock's blowers start up, flushing out the water. The Ren'kari kept its song masked.

Mon wondered if any Ren'kari had ever come inside. They were amphibious, so why not?

Power play. Dare the fragile human to brave the pressure of a real ocean.

Olve was back by the time the airlock had flushed, less than a minute. This time, Aster was with him. Between them they carried something heavy and big, like a duffel full of NutriBars.

They wrenched open the airlock and dropped the thing on the floor with a thud. Olve retrieved the still-wet tablet and closed the door. As soon as the air lock cycled, the Ren'kari ambassador retrieved the package, lifting it effortlessly and holding it in one arm, and departed.

But Olve didn't stop cursing, or growling.

Aster rushed to Mon, hand held out for the tablet.

They recognized the map at a glance.

"Shit," Aster said. "It's Apple City."

Chapter Eight

Olve threw himself into the chair at the end of the large meeting table so hard it pushed back half a meter, even though it wasn't on wheels. He started to run his fingers through his tangled hair, but stopped, gripping his head instead.

"Starsdammit all! They've known for days." he said. "And they weren't going to tell us."

Aster, still looking at the tablet screen with the map and exact coordinates, held up a single finger: hold that thought. A moment later, they set the tablet on the table.

"I've sent the alert, and all the data," they said. "Small human population, luckily. Too bad about all the apple trees. But why such short notice?"

"I just told you, starsdammit! They weren't going to tell us at all. They were holding the information for ransom, for their shipment."

Aster's face contorted through horror, anger, confusion.

"But how were we supposed to know that?" they said. "They didn't threaten us."

"Maybe they did." Olve threw his head backwards, banging the base of his skull on the top of the chair. Once, twice.

Mon winced.

That spot behind her ear pinged again. Mon looked at Aster. They had their hand pressed to their forehead, staring at the shiny black tabletop.

She checked her wristcom.

Heather.

Probably just got Mon's message.

Nobody noticed Mon stepping away from the table, toward the hall door. She opened the link.

"Hey, kid," she said.

"Mon! I cannot believe they let you go underwater! And you didn't even come see me first."

Heather never needed coffee.

"Sorry," Mon said. "Command performance. But I'll stop by next I can."

"I sent a message to get that scanner to you," Heather said. Her voice sounded so much happier than back at Smithson Station. "You would not believe what we just did!"

"You wouldn't believe what we just did, either."

"We moved five thousand people, and everything in their houses. And most of their houses, too. And hospitals and all the vehicles. In two days! They go supra modular with design here. And you know what? Nobody screamed or got upset. Everybody works together here. It's so weird. Good weird, you know?"

"I heard they could do that. And you saw it?"

"I helped! I Listened as we dismantled and packed up all the power and comms lines. I knew one line wasn't powered down yet. And they paid attention to me! And fixed it! I learned all about infrastructure. Ask me anything." Mon could just picture Heather helping. Her long hair—probably a new color again—tied up. Her favorite coveralls with the flower patches on the pockets. Her grape-drink lips.

"I'm so glad," she said. "You're hyperspeed."

"It's supersonic, duh." As Heather continued to regale Mon with tales of the evacuation, Mon's gaze drifted back to Olve and Aster, hunched over the waterproof tablet, pointing and grumbling, their faces etched with concentration and frustration.

"... and I think the scanner you asked for should be on its way soon," Heather was saying, pulling Mon's attention back to the conversation. "Maybe already. I don't have it with me, but my friend ArVee Six says he knows where it is and can overnight it. Unless it's an emergency. Is it an emergency? I can go on the chats and request expedition."

"It might be an emergency—but wait! Let us ask for things to be expedited. You need to be helping, not asking for special favors. Where are you now?"

"Not sure. We're all in these fast sailboats, you know, the rescuers. On our way to another island. Don't want to be a drag on the people getting settled in, you know? We're going to a place with hot springs and not much else. Just farms, and lots of fruit, and a big dock."

Off-mic, Heather said, "Where are we going, again?" Then her voice came back. "Oh yeah, right. Fruit. It's called Apple Island."

Of all places.

"Sorry kid," she said. "No rest for you yet."

Chapter Nine

Mon doublechecked her comm, making sure the call was off. She jammed her hands into the soft pockets of the sweater Heather had sent and paced back to the table. It wasn't that cold in the lab, or anywhere in the underwater base, so long as you kept moving. She just liked the soft braids of the weave. And the sky-blue joy of the color. And the thought that Heather had chosen it just for her.

While she'd been trying to catch up with Heather, Aster and Olve had raided Olve's castle and brought their booty to the long meeting table. Now the surface held quite a few of those palm-sized black boxes that could be anything but in this case were data processors and screens.

One screen already was up, displaying waveforms in the spectrum that humans use for sound. Another screen popped up data on chemical scans of the Ren'kari taken during earlier meetings. A third and fourth were teamed to process ranges of luminescence.

Olve was actually sharing data. He'd ceded a great deal of territory.

He really must be desperate.

"Wow," Mon said. "So much. You've done a lot already." Stroke the cranky colleague.

He shrugged, all false modesty.

Then she ruined it.

"Any progress?" she said, peering at the structure of an algorithm that was trying to match bioluminescent pulses and vibrational frequencies.

Olve drooped, frustration etched into the lines of his face. He pushed his hair back again. A miracle the man wasn't bald.

"It's like trying to crack a code within a code within a code, without even one of the keys," he said. "We've tried every linguistic analysis method known to Arkhide—and to the Realm—but nothing fits."

Aster stood up as the screen linked to the black box he was fussing with came to life. It seemed to hold the collection of recordings, video and probably basic human-range audio.

"We do know it's a multi-modal communication system," they said. "Like the dance dialects of honey bees or the ultrasonic songs of whales. Like us, even. But with the added complexity of bioluminescence and chemical signaling."

Mon studied the patterns on one screen and then the next. These systems were all siloed. Why weren't they talking with one another?

"What about a cross-modal approach?" she said. "Like how people figured out dolphin whistles?"

Olve waved at the screens. "Tried, failed. And so has every other method you can think of. Trust me, if there was a way, we would have found it."

Mon bristled at Olve's dismissive tone, but forced herself to remain calm.

"So now you've brought in outside help," she said. "Maybe it's worth it to take another look."

Olve crossed his arms.

"So. Look."

Aster sighed audibly.

Mon released the exasperation she had been holding in with one long silent out-breath and sank into the chair at the opposite end from Olve. The screens could show be able to show any cube's data so it didn't matter where she sat.

She called up her wristcom's interface.

"That thing's going to slow you down," Olve said.

"I'm not implanted." This interface was what she had.

Olve snorted.

"Hey, Olve," Aster said before Mon had a chance to open her mouth. "Did you have breakfast? How about we get some. You can leave Mon here with that last report, the one you loaded on the group chat last week? That's a good breakdown of what we know."

Olve thought it over, glowering.

"Fine," he said. "We'll get some and bring it in." He looked at her. "You didn't eat yet either, right?"

"NutriBar."

His face reflected her own poor opinion of the bars. He pushed to his feet. He was so thin he looked like he should get a breakfast, lunch, and dinner.

"Something warm, then," he said.

Aster reached for his friend and started shepherding him toward the door.

"Report's in your workspace," Olve said as he headed out the door.

The report was among the many Olve had dumped into her online workspace yesterday. But now he'd tagged it, so it popped to the top.

Mon opened the file and dove into the dense text and complex diagrams. She loved puzzles.

The report was an omnibus, detailing the various methods and tools the team had used to analyze the Ren'kari language and methods of communication over the past 23 years.

One section described the use of a specialized underwater acoustic array, designed to capture the full range of the Ren'kari's vocal communication. The array, composed of hundreds of hydrophones and accelerometers, helped researchers create detailed 3D maps of the soundscape, revealing intricate patterns and structures.

Another section of the report focused on the team's efforts to decode the Ren'kari's bioluminescent signaling. Researchers had developed a high-speed, high-resolution camera system capable of capturing the rapid flashes and pulses of light emitted by the Ren'kari. Using new image processing algorithms, they were able to identify distinct patterns and sequences in the light displays, hinting at a complex visual grammar.

She'd reached the section on chemical signaling when she smelled the pancakes. Aster and Olve both carried trays; Aster's was the one with the mouthwatering scent.

"Come and sit right by me," Mon said to them, patting the seat of the chair next to her.

"Oh, no," Aster said grinning. "I'm not playing favorites." They set a round plate that really did not look that different from the thousand-year-old one on the display shelf in front of her. This one, though, had three perfectly square pancakes. No melted sugar, though. Arkhideans apparently preferred fruit.

Aster set a similar plate at Olve's spot, and one at their own.

"You eat, too?" popped out of Mon's mouth before she thought better of it.

"Oh, yes," Aster said. "Eating's one of my favorite things. But you're right. Not all of us need food as sustenance. Even me—I could swap out my stomach for power cells if I absolutely had to." They shrugged. "But what fun would that be?"

Olve's contribution to breakfast was more delightful coffee and the cutlery she needed for the pancakes.

Mon speared one of the slices of fruit. It looked sweet, and crunchy.

"Apple," Olve said. "We get a lot of it, because Apple Island isn't far from here."

The thought of Apple Island, and its imminent danger, killed all conversation for a while.

"Are we safe?" Mon said.

"The Ren'kari chose this place for us because it was so stable," Aster said. The fault and flow affecting Apple Island is on its other side from us."

Mon almost didn't hear them. The sweet tartness of the apple and its sauce on the soft warm pancake took all her attention for a good few minutes. With her stomach digesting happily, Mon turned back to the report.

The chemical signaling aspect of the Ren'kari's communication had proven most challenging. The team had used an array of sensitive chemical sensors and mass spectrometers to detect and analyze the various compounds released by the Ren'kari during their interactions. The water pressure had been particularly hard on these sensors. While researchers had managed to catalog a wide range of chemical signals, no one could yet say what they meant.

No one could yet say what most of the rest of it meant, either.

The team had used machine learning techniques to try to integrate the disparate modes of communication. They fed their vast amounts of acoustic, visual, and chemical data into these deep neural networks, hoping to uncover hidden correlations and patterns. While the different models had produced some intriguing insights, none of them cracked the code.

The team had even experimented with interactive language learning paradigms, using specially designed underwater drones to engage with the Ren'kari in real-time. These drones, equipped with speakers, lights, and chemical emitters, allowed them to mimic and respond to the Ren'kari's various signaling methods.

The Ren'kari had sent those back in pieces inside two of the shipping kegs.

"Do you still have those interactive drones?" Mon said.

"Don't ask," Aster said.

"I told them not to do it," Olve glowered. He crunched an apple slice, scowling. "But I was just the trainee then."

Perhaps the most ambitious approach the research teams had taken had stretched the whole of the lab's twenty-three-year history. They were trying to hand-code a basic codex for the gestures used in the language. They hoped creating a database of Ren'kari signals and their associated contexts would help them find map communication modes and content to observable behaviors or environmental factors.

This monumental effort had revealed tantalizing glimpses of structure and meaning, but the sheer complexity and variability of the Ren'kari language had defeated them. So far.

Mon searched for the Codex. It lived on two of its own little black boxes. A dictionary for a language that nobody human understood.

As Mon reached the end of the report, a summary paragraph caught her eye:

"It is clear that the Ren'kari possess a rich, nuanced language that is deeply embedded in their unique sensory experiences and cultural context. Deciphering this language will require not only further technological advancements but also a paradigm shift in our approach to interspecies communication.

"We must strive to see the world through the Ren'kari's eyes, to understand the fundamental concepts and metaphors that shape their perception of reality. Only then can we hope to truly grasp the essence of their language and forge a meaningful dialogue between our species."

Mon thought of the young Ren'kari she'd met today. Who better to see the world anew than a teenager?

Heather.

She picked up her now-empty coffee mug and moved down the table to sit at Aster's right. They had the thermal coffee pot in front of them. They poured out another sweet dose for her.

Mon lifted the mug, just sniffing, not drinking.

"You don't think Coffee Island is in danger, do you?"

Aster laughed. Even Olve snorted.

"Coffee is grown on at least four of our islands," Aster said. "And apples on two, don't worry about them."

"Makes sense," Mon said. "I want to tell you a little bit about me."

Well, that sure sounded like a non sequitur. But it made Aster giggle.

"Hey, that's my line. Hey, Mon, tell us a little bit about yourself."

She smiled, and then grew serious.

"I'm a Listener. I'm not sure you know what that means. We're rare, and nobody knows why we can do what we do."

Olve leaned forward. His eyes were starting to droop, even with all the caffeine in his system.

"Which is, what?" he said.

"We call it Listening, but we don't do it with our ears." She frowned. "Well, not exactly. It really does feel mostly like hearing, but it isn't really sound. Maybe our minds call it sound because we don't have another word for it. Anyway, what really good Listeners can do is hear the made world. Power grids. Ship engines. Satellite transmissions—but we can't hear the words just that they're transmitting. Everything made makes a sound."

Aster stared at her.

"That's... a lot of noise," they said.

"We develop ways to manage it."

Olve's gaze flicked to Mon's face.

"Is that why the coconut ears?"

She'd forgotten she was still wearing the noise-canceling headphones. She pulled them off, heat rising to her face.

"Yes. This is my friend Heather's invention. It blocks most known Listener-only sounds. I can still hear you, and music and stuff. But with these on, I wouldn't know that right now someone is using the stove in the kitchen."

Aster touched one of the half-spheres of the headphones.

"Heather Quostov?" At Mon's expression of surprise, they continued. "Hers was the other Listener we were debating on the forums. She's a pistol! But too young."

"I agreed with that decision." Not to mention that Heather would have run screaming from Olve the first day. She was the age of the normal intern, and not yet used to putting up with asshole bosses. "But now I'm not so sure."

She offered the phones to Aster, who took them eagerly. As they looked at them in and out, Mon considered how to say the next part.

"The Ren'kari are a riot of sound in the Listener spectrum," she said. "I had to wear the phones today to block normal noise so I could use my mental training to try to block out the Ren'kari."

Olve's spine straightened, like a meerkat sighting dinner.

"Explain," he said. "I know you 'sensed' something yesterday when Zhi'laris was approaching. The ambassador."

"It was as if a symphony orchestra was playing while riding on a parade float, coming nearer. And then, just before they came into view, it damped way down. And then," she waved a hand in frustration. "That shout. You heard it?"

"The ambassador's honk?" Olve said.

"Good word for it," Aster agreed.

"That had a different set of harmonics with it. And, maybe colors. Luminescence. But I'm not sure about that part."

Olve's mouth twisted, but not in anger.

"We'd need a Seer, capital S, for that," quipped Aster.

"Keep trying, Aster," Olve said.

"Anyway," Mon said. "Heather is sending me one of the scanners she uses to fix on new sounds that affect Listeners. It's a finicky tool, as you might imagine. First the Listener has to hear a new, usually horrible, sound. Then they sit with this machine, tuning wavelengths, impedances, whatever, over and over until they find something that affects the sound. Worst thing is when that something reinforces the sound, because it usually bumps it up logarithmically."

Everybody winced.

"But once we have that link," Mon said, "Heather can rejigger her algorithm to dampen that one, too."

"Like whack-a-stole," Aster said.

"Stop trying, Aster." Olve said. To Mon, he said, "So you think this machine will be able to find these, whatever, frequencies? When we couldn't?"

Mon shrugged. "Do you hear the Ren'kari when they're near?"

Aster pressed their lips together.

Olve leaned back and scowled. And then seemed to reconsider.

"Couldn't hurt." He shrugged. "Except you, I guess."

"Thanks," Mon said.

Chapter Ten

When the Base Six daily shipment came in the next morning, Olve and Mon were in the lab. Olve sat at the near end of the long meeting table, glowering at the screen in front of him. It showed the black box's progress working through a new algorithm trying to match the Ren'kari light patterns to the meaning of their gestures.

Mon, halfway down the table on the near side, so she could see the water, was also running a tweaked algorithm. Hers hoped to match the vocal sounds to light patterns. But she had that screen dimmed. If she didn't stare at it, maybe it would work this time.

Heather's Listening device was on its way, coming today or tomorrow. The Ren'kari weren't expected anytime soon, but Mon really wanted her hands on that device before they appeared again.

Olve looked like he hadn't slept, again, but at least he had showered. His hair lay straight down the back of his head and just onto his collarbone. Mon's hair was that long, too, if straight. But in this humidity it was the opposite of straight. So kinky she was afraid even to brush it. She'd tamed it, somewhat, into two braids flat on her head, but what she really needed was a bandanna to just smoosh the whole of it out of sight.

Resolutely not looking at her working screen, she instead focused on the smaller one, which showed how to indicate tenses in Galactic Sign Language. But her mind wasn't really on it.

She paused the screen and turned to look at Olve.

"You know," she said, "You could help me with the GSL. It would be more efficient."

"Don't need you to know GSL," Olve said, not taking his eyes off his screen. "Nothing to listen to in that modality."

Freaking obtuse coral-head.

"But if I could use it, as a bridge. Like, you know, we're trying to do with all this algorithming, it might help."

Olve looked at her then. His eyes seemed to pulse. The skin on his cheeks sagged.

He really hadn't slept.

Mon quelled the impulse to reach for his hand. This guy needed some comfort. She toned her sarcasm down and her sympathy up.

"You okay?" she said.

He looked away from her, towards the water. He ran his hands through his hair so tightly he probably pressed water onto the back of his black T-shirt. It was so warm in here that even though Mon had switched to T-shirt and ankle slacks today, she was still moist. Surely this heat couldn't be just from all the processors grinding away.

"What if they hadn't told us?" Olve said, staring at the sea. Probably seeing the Ren'kari in his mind. "If they let our people die? And then more people? And more?"

He dropped his hands into his lap. He looked down at them.

"What did I do? What mistake did I make?"

Mon frowned. Why was he blaming himself? It was the supplies that were late.

"Wasn't the problem the kegs?" she said.

He shook his head so hard his shoulders shook. Needed some muscle on those bones. Or fat. Or anything.

"This is just the latest. I've been sensing—feeling—noticing something..." He stopped.

She waited for him to work through his thoughts.

"Impatience," he said. "I think."

"The Ren'kari are impatient?" she said neutrally. Mirroring, not confirming.

He nodded once. He glanced at her.

"Or bored. Whatever. Done with us."

That didn't make any sense. "But don't they need the trade?"

He waved his hand, dismissing the idea.

"Servos could do that. And we have enough of the language—nouns and numbers and the idea of day and night—to make that work."

Mon sighed audibly, hoping that would remind Olve to take a breath.

"See, the thing is," he said. He looked at her with his sad, sleepy eyes. "The Ren'kari, they're not that interested in us."

"In humans?"

"Right. Zhi'laris told me the other day. They said, the other humans were better. Not sure the word was better, but it was positive for them and not to us."

"The humans they kicked off the planet?" Mon couldn't keep the surprise out of her voice.

Olve's gaze turned bleak. "They killed them. All."

Mon's hand went to her throat.

"Killed them? Or let them die?"

"Killed them. Came up in dark, took the human's own tools, apparently. Killed them all."

That didn't usually stop humans, in Mon's experience.

"Wouldn't other ones come, then?" she said.

Olve shrugged. He glanced at his screen, and then away. Must be still running the algorithm.

"Zhi'laris said the other humans weren't as interested in chatting. Like that was a good thing."

"The Ren'kari don't like small talk?"

Olve pushed to his feet. The pacing started again. Most researchers Mon knew paced, but in thought, not to release steam. Olve stomped to the window. And punched it.

"They don't want to have anything to do with us!" he said. He rested his forehead on the glass.

Mon was up and at the window in a flash. No damage to the window, thank the stars.

All Olve's damage was previous to the punch.

She touched his shoulder, and then rested her hand on it. What had Aster said, the last time?

"Have you eaten lately?"

Olve groaned and turned out of her grasp. He slammed his back into the glass, and then sank to the floor. He set his elbows on his upraised knees and covered his eyes with the palms of his hands. His hands were so pretty, so long and tapered, but his nails were bitten to the quick.

Mon crouched beside him. She was missing something. Olve blamed himself for whatever miscommunication was happening lately. The Ren'kari didn't want to communicate in the first place.

Ah.

"So it's like with me," she said. "If you helped, I could learn GSL faster. But you think I don't need to learn it. If the Ren'kari helped, we'd know their languages by now But they don't think we need to know."

Olve didn't lift his head. "What if I pushed them too hard? I thought—I still think—we could give so much to them. To each other."

Now he lifted his head, to bash the back of it on the window.

Mon reminded herself that the window was tougher than it looked. The thought didn't stop the panic-glance at the glass again. It was fine.

The question slipped out.

"Then, why are we here?" The Ren'kari were allowed their privacy. One could not be forced to socialize. Every being had the right to autonomy.

Olve was not tougher than he looked. His gaze at her carried the pain of betrayal.

"You, too?" he said, voice choking.

"No," she said, comfortingly. She didn't know what she was saying no to. Maybe just the despair in his eyes.

The hall door slid open.

"Package for Mondrian Delacroix!" Aster said.

They paused for a moment, taking in the scene. Then they rushed to crouch at Olve's other side.

"Algorithm didn't work?" they said, their face clearly hoping it was something as simple as that.

When Olve didn't answer, or even look at them, Aster looked at Mon. Their face lost that last trace of a smile.

They handed her a small package, a homemade tie-dyed cloth bag with a shoelace tie.

The Listening device.

She loosened the tie and pulled the thing out. It looked like every other small tablet, except for the three extra mini-satellite dishes plugged into one end. She turned it on and opened a floating screen. The familiar grids came up.

But no data.

Mon fiddled with the frequency controls. Then the impedance. Nothing.

She looked across Olve, at Aster. Both were staring at the quiet, empty grid on the screen.

"Told you it wouldn't work," Olve said.

Before Mon could react to that, Aster reached for the device. Mon handed it to them.

Using their two right hands, Aster lifted it to the light, turning it this way and that. Peering into one of the tiny openings in the device.

"What's it use for a membrane?"

What would Heather have had access to? Mon racked her brain.

"Rubber?"

"Won't work down here." Aster nodded, thinking. "We see that a lot, as Olve so rudely put it." They looked up, at Mon. "Easy fix."

"Come with me."

Chapter Eleven

Mon followed Aster down the main hall and back to the elevators at the entrance. Behind the left elevator was a thick metal door that led to a hidden staircase. Well, hidden if you didn't know to look for it.

Mon grasped the cold metal railing of the stairwell, each step resonating softly against the rough-hewn gray stone walls. The scent of salt and metal were a constant reminder of the ocean's presence.

"Aster, could I ask you a personal question?" she said.

"No I don't dye my hair." At Mon's look of complete confusion, they laughed. "Okay, you got me. I do color my hair."

She didn't know what to say. "It's a nice shade?"

"Brown 56b. B for extra body," they said, shaking their head. The short-buzzed hair didn't move.

"Right," she said. "Well, yes. It is about your body."

"Moi?" At the first of the stairwell landings, they struck a pose, hips canted, bottom arms on hips, top arms up, hands in their hair.

They were not making this easier. She stopped on the landing.

"So, I'm a Listener, right?" she said. "I sense stuff that's usually outside human senses. I think that means I can hear you."

She stopped, and started again. "I mean, of course I can hear you, but I mean I think I could identify you with my eyes closed. But I'm not sure. So I'm wondering."

Aster dropped their top arms onto their hips in front of their bottom arms.

"Not sure," they said, slow, "I can help you with that."

Mon frowned. How to say it better?

She tried again. "I've only met two—three—synthetic humans. Aimee Five overwhelms me with her scent."

"Aimee Five terrifies all wise sentients," Aster said.

"And Allen Eleven hums from his belly," Mon pushed on. "And you, you—"

"I?"

Mon shook her head in exasperation.

"You are a combination of sounds," she said. "Sound-senses. But, you see, I don't know if it is you or if it is all synthetic humans."

Aster pursed their lips.

"Probably just all Asters."

That made sense.

"How many Asters are there?" she said.

"One." They winked. This time they struck the hands-on-chin pose.

Mon couldn't believe what she was about to say.

"I wish there were more synths here. So I could compare. For science."

Curiosity must have overcome her fear. For now. Plus, her feelings about synths might be changing. All the synths she'd met had been more people than evil killing machines.

All three of them.

Aster's face lit up. They broke their pose and started taking the next set of stairs two at a time.

"Oh! Wait till you see the cargo cave! Everybody else has been down here for three days. More than half our staff is synths."

What?

As Mon reached the bottom, going one stair at a time, the echo of her footsteps faded, replaced by the low hum of the base's systems. The cave's acoustics amplified the burrs of the HVAC system and the air blowers, and the flows of power and water lines up to the lab level.

Stepping onto the stone landing, she had to sit on a stair and catch her breath. Stupid pressure, making her feel old. The two square metal cargo elevators stood silent to her left, their doors closed. She'd asked to take the stairs, needing the movement to shake off the stiffness in her knees and work out some simmering exasperation. Now if she could just have a little more oxygen.

She and the elevators faced a double-wide airlock, not just a simple thick door like up on the main base level. Both sets of the airlock's metallic doors were wide open, showing the dim cave beyond.

Should have brought her sweater.

Mon pushed herself up and stepped through the doors. And stopped again.

The vast, shadowy space felt half-finished and a little creepy. Her eyes struggled to adjust to the dim lighting, a jarring mix of the usual artificial blue-white strips along the walls just above head height and a murky green glow emanating from... was that actual water?

She took a step back, touching the frame of the airlock door. Time to run?

But Aster was standing right next to her, not worried at all.

Mon shook her head—soldier up!—and stepped back out.

The cave stretched out before her, a long box but with an odd steep slope of a floor. Luckily the black rubber carpet-stuff grabbed at her feet. No slipping here.

But she couldn't stop staring at the green pool of water at the far end of the cave, right where a wide arch led to the sea. The opening must be blocked; she could see the water beyond through some clear window material. But the level of the pool didn't rise to meet it. It stayed at floor height.

Mon blinked in disbelief. Shouldn't the cave be flooded?

Apparently not.

In the pool, close to the far wall of the cave, floated one of those turtle seacraft. It took up one-third of the pool. Round and with four flipper-rudders, the rover's controls and seats were visible through its transparent cover. Pretty standard-looking.

Behind the rover stood the lift-crane and a rover-recharge platform. Balanced on mismatched legs to make a flat surface above the steep bank of the cave floor, the platform was wide enough for two rovers.

Someone must be out and about.

Racks of wetsuits, tanks, and other diving gear hung on the wall to her right.

To her left, four wide white ceramic-coated metal workbenches sat on a series of stepped platforms perpendicular to the wall. On the wall itself, on the usual long multipurpose wood-like boards with hooks, hung the contents of an entire tool shed. The familiar sight of tools and equipment grounded her somewhat, even if the painted-pink wall behind them seemed a tad whimsical.

An arm's length away on her right ranged a half-dozen giant metal standing shelves, big enough to hold scores of Ren'kari-sized kegs. Only two of the two-meter-tall kegs rested there now. There was the problem, larger than life.

Something big and grindery rumbled beyond the wall. That,

and a squishy sound, like the water tanks on a troop ship. Must be the clean room with the mixers that made the green gel.

Near the kegs, the sweet aroma of summer grass overwhelmed the soggy, salt-tinged air. Mon inhaled deeply. Lovely.

Aster beelined for the only person visible, at one of the middle workbenches. This synthetic human also preferred shades of pink: hair, nails, even skin.

"Floyd!" Aster started to lean an elbow on their workbench. The pink synth swung a hand holding some pointy tool toward Aster and waggled it with each word.

"Don't. Jiggle. The table. Drape yourself elsewhere."

Aster mock-pouted. "But what if you don't see me?"

The smaller synth finished whatever they were doing, sighed, and looked up at Aster. Even the pupils of their eyes were a blushing pink, prettily offset by the white.

"Not a chance," they said, and smiled. They had cornered the market on hot pink lipstick.

Aster tipped their head back, toward Mon. "Mon, here, needs our help." They turned to look at Mon. "Floyd, here, is our lead engineer and Jane-of-all-trades. Ask her anything."

Mon looked from Floyd to the pool of water to her right and back to Floyd. "So, why aren't we all wet?"

This time, Floyd grinned. "Never seen a moon pool?"

Floyd set down her tool and swiveled on her stool to face Mon fully. "Simple concept. Clever execution."

Aster bounced on their toes. "Oh, can I explain it? Pretty please?"

Floyd rolled her eyes but waved a hand for Aster to take over.

Aster cleared their throat theatrically. "Picture, if you will, a magical doorway to the ocean right beneath our feet!" They swept an arm toward the pool. "The moon pool is nature's very own airlock, allowing us land-dwellers to commune with the watery depths without turning our cozy cave into an impromptu aquarium!"

Not convincing. "How?" Mon said.

"Air pressure," Floyd said. "Keeps the water at bay."

Aster mock-frowned at Floyed. "Ahem. My line."

Floyd snorted.

"It's a delicate dance between air and water, my friend," Aster said. "The air in this cave, trapped by these walls of sturdy stone even sturdier polymer, pushes down on the water's surface." They mimed pressing down with both hands. "Meanwhile, the ocean outside pushes back, creating a perfect equilibrium at the pool's edge."

Floyd stood up, stretching. "Reverse diving bell."

"Ooh, good analogy!" Aster beamed. "I'll add it to the patter, for our next land-lubber."

"Thinking I'll stick closer to you, Floyd," Mon said. "No reason to tempt fate."

"Perfectly engineered," Floyd said. "Multiple failsafes. No worries."

"Sure." Mon stepped down to the level of Floyd's table and handed the synth Heather's scanner.

"Help?" she said. "It turns on, but doesn't scan."

Floyd sussed its workings in no time. She turned it on and projected its screen. A screen just as empty of data as it had been back in the lab.

"Pressure EQ fail, I bet," Floyd said "That's the jigger what makes the internal pressure match external pressure."

"Right," Mon said. "But it worked in vacuum."

Floyd snorted. "No pressure, there." She turned the device in her hands. She had only two arms, but it looked like she might be able to replace her hands at the wrists. Whatever she'd done to her ruby shoulder-length hair, it did not swing into her way. She carried a faint smell of lubricant and roses mixed with the earthy scent of the cave walls.

"Whoever made this bashed a couple of scanners and maybe even another comms piece all together in here," she said. "Fine job, but gotta be touchy."

"Finicky, yes," Mon said. "But sensitive things often are."

"There you go, talking about me again," Aster said. "But can you fix it?"

Floyd snorted. "Child's play."

She spread a rubbery looking mat on her already clean table and opened the casing of the device. Using the same sharp tool she'd fended Aster off with, she flicked out two tiny pieces.

"Synthesized rubber," she said, stabbing one with the tiny awl and holding it up to Mon. "Good choice for spacer work, but shit for down this deep. Get this a lot. Should have just shipped it direct to me."

She turned toward the table behind her, which held a coral-colored wooden box with many little drawers. She squatted down to that table's level, and pulled out two drawers. Floyd turned and held up two different materials, one dark, the other glossy.

"Replace with carbon nanotube-reinforced polymer, or graphene-based composite? Advantage to graphene is it will still work in space."

"Why didn't Heather use that, then?" asked Mon, surprised.

"I know that one," Aster said. "Way more expensive. And overkill, see? Synthetic rubber would be good enough for almost anywhere."

Heather hadn't known her tool would be needed at the bottom of the ocean. No surprise, there. No one had.

Mon nodded. "How do you have these materials to share, then?"

Aster laughed. The cave walls and water trumpeted back their mirth.

"Who says we're sharing? I'm taking it out of your pay."

Mon frowned. "I'm getting paid?"

That made Aster laugh harder.

"Told you," they said to Floyd, who had returned to the site of scanner surgery. "She came because she was needed, not because Aimee bribed her."

Floyd, concentrating on the device, clicked a lamp on to see it better.

"Captain Delacroix," Floyd said, not looking at her. "We did vote to pay you something, before Aimee even offered you the job. Check the feeds. Don't let anyone tell you otherwise. And we will not charge you for fixing a tool that we desperately need."

"Spoilsport," Aster said.

Floyd smiled at the device. "What's the movie tonight?"

"Not 'Mecha-Dance Dream 3,' if that's what you're asking."

Floyd clicked the outer casing back into place.

"There. Try now." She handed it to Mon.

Mon powered on the device again, bringing up the floating screen. This time, data flowed into the basic display.

"Jammed in both a CNRP membrane and a graphene composite," Floyd said with satisfaction. "Redundancy is bliss."

Aster grinned at her. "And you know we're going to be using this baby a lot."

The basic scan cycled through the most-common spectrums, placing what it heard on a simple graph of the space. Mon saw the HVAC system, the power conduits, the comms conduits. Dots representing Floyd and Aster also appeared.

They did, indeed, have slightly different signature wavelengths and overtones. Chords, Mon's brain called them.

Aster leaned in, pointing at the dot that showed them.

"Hey, that's me! And you!" They pointed at the dot representing Floyd. Aster looked away from the screen and around the room. "But there should be two more."

"And another rover," Floyd said. "Took your time noticing. Twins went off in the main turtle to see if they got the rudders right this time."

Aster sighed theatrically. "Might not have been a good idea to completely dismantle it just to see if they could put it back together again," they said.

"Weren't anything else for them to do," Floyd countered. "Besides sit around waiting for kegs. Gotta fix the supply chain."

"I'm working on it."

Mon rolled through the various wavelengths on the device, reminding herself how it worked. She blocked first Aster's signal, and then Floyd's.

"Where'd we go?" Floyd said.

"Blocked your signal, just yours," Mon said. "That's how we confirm the wavelengths." She untuned the device, and both Aster's and Floyd's dots reappeared. "Once we have that, we can add that block to our headphones."

"And then you won't hear us all the time, like now?" Aster said.

"Who would want to?" Floyd said.

"Exactly," Mon said. "To the first part, I mean." She pointed at a single dot. "Which twin is that?"

"Wouldn't be single," Floyd said, peering at the screen.

The single dot, outside the room, moved closer.

"And where's the rover?" Floyd said. "That square is the one right here, right?"

"Must be out of range?" Mon started to say, and stopped. Some of the overtones of Ren'kari were growing louder. But only some.

The dot had almost reached the pool.

Floyd set her tiny awl down and lifted a giant wrench from the wall. On her small frame, the wrench looked out-of-proportion big. But she seemed just as adept at wielding it, her grip confident and steady.

"Might be a friend," Aster said.

"Might not," said Floyd.

All three stared into the shadowed pool.

A brighter shadow shot past the outer edge of the pool. It stopped in the center so fast the water around it swirled like a whirlpool. The flickers on the wall and ceiling swirled in eerie sympathy.

Out of the water, the tippy-tippiest of a gray carapace lifted.

The little Ren'kari.

For a moment, the three on land and the one in the water just looked at each other.

Then the Ren'kari in the water made the sign for hello.

Chapter Twelve

Mon walked to the edge of the pool, her eyes fixed on the little Ren'kari. The cargo cave's damp chill had burned away in the blaze of excitement that coursed through her.

The little Ren'kari's segmented exoskeleton pulsed blue, green, purple pink. Stable, not worried, Mon figured.

Really? How did she know?

Maybe through her Listening—the Ren'kari's braided harmonies rang stable and consistent. Or the colors—like the ambassador's, who was always in control. Or something else?

The Ren'kari's upper limbs coasted through the water, fluid and graceful. As they approached the pool's pressed-stone edge, six kegs bobbed up to the top of the water behind them.

"Odd," Aster said, coming up behind Mon. "Usually we come down here, and the kegs are already sitting on the shelves, waiting. Or if we've filled the kegs up, the next morning they are gone. Figured the Ren'kari knew our work schedule and didn't want to bother saying hi."

But this Ren'kari had brazenly brought the kegs in full view of everyone.

Mon's mind buzzed with questions. What had prompted this change in behavior? Was it a sign of trust? Desperation?

The Ren'kari grabbed the first keg and pushed it toward the lip of the pool. There was a short shelf about a half-meter below the pool's edge, giving the little Ren'kari good leverage.

Aster and Floyd, who had dropped her wrench and crept closer, sprang forward. Aster pulled the first one in and used all four hands to carry it to the room behind the tall shelves. Floyd took the next, rolling it instead of carrying it. As soon as the third came up, Aster was back. The whole haul took less than five minutes.

Mon's attention snapped back to the Ren'kari. The little thing, colors flashing down their back, didn't seem to be slinking away. They floated at top of the water. Their big oval eyes, swirling silver, aimed at Mon.

Mon left the Listening device on and jammed it into a side pocket to free her hands. Looking at the Ren'kari, she signed hello. Trying to be simple and clear, she followed that with the signs that they should go up and meet her at the lab.

Olve would want to see this.

But the Ren'kari signed no, their bioluminescent patterns flickering with what Mon could only interpret as reluctance. Instead, they pulled themself up onto the ledge just below the pool's edge, keeping the lower part of their exoskeleton and most of their limbs submerged.

Their soft triangle of a carapace glistened.

In human space.

Mon reeled. The Ren'kari were amphibious, sure, but could they really stand the special air mix the humans needed down here? What if they were allergic to helium?

What had compelled this one to take such a risk?

The Ren'kari's scent grew stronger as they settled on the ledge, a strange but not unpleasant aroma that reminded Mon of a warm ocean breeze tinged with sweet corn.

Guess they were staying, then.

Mon looked to Aster, who had returned from the refilling room.

"Call Olve?" she said. "Ask him to come down. And bring those waterproof comms screens."

Mon approached slowly, hopefully unthreateningly, and sat down a short-tentacle-length away from the Ren'kari. Without thinking, she set her booted feet on the underwater ledge. The shocking chill stole inside, freezing her feet and sending a shiver up her spine. The chill of the metal ledge contrasted with the warmth emanating from the Ren'kari's luminous form.

With the Ren'kari mostly on the lower shelf and Mon up a step up, their eyes were almost at the same level. Humans must look so dull to them, with no lights on their body anywhere.

The intricacy of their exoskeleton amazed her. Up close, Mon could see the finer details—the iridescent sheen, gray now but edging in places into the translucent that made up the ambassador's shell. Delicate ridges ringed the top of the shell. Pulsing bioluminescence seemed to respond to every movement.

A soft, melodic sound emanated from the Ren'kari, a gentle hum that seemed to vibrate through Mon's very bones. It was a far cry from the discordant, overwhelming sensations she had experienced earlier, and Mon found herself leaning closer, drawn in by the almost hypnotic quality of this alien presence.

"Do you hear that?" she asked Aster and Floyd, still near the wall behind her. "The humming?"

Silence from them suggested no.

"Sorry," Aster whispered.

The Ren'kari tilted their head, their multifaceted eyes glinting in the blue-tinted light. Were they sizing her up?

Mon wanted to touch their shell, or their arm. Would it be stiff or supple?

For sure, it would cause a diplomatic incident. She kept her hands on her knees, gripping hard.

A moment later, the Ren'kari raised one of their smaller, front limbs and began to move it in a series of complex gestures.

It took Mon a moment to realize what she was seeing.

The Ren'kari was finger-spelling. In Galactic.

Their slender limb, especially the three segments at its tip, moved with surprising dexterity. The light patterns along the limb pulsed in a steady, mesmerizing rhythm. Mon wished she knew what the lights were adding to the conversation.

"A... R... apostrophe... A... S... H... A," Mon spelled out, her voice a whisper. "Ar'asha. She."

The Ren'kari signed yes, her multifaceted eyes shimmering with what Mon could only interpret as approval. Her underwater limbs swirled in agreement.

How long had Ar'asha had been studying human language? And where?

Mon raised her own hands, finger-spelling her name in return. She pointed to herself, then repeated the gesture, emphasizing each letter.

Ar'asha mimicked the movement, her three "fingers" forming the letters with surprising accuracy.

Mon had to tell Olve the Ren'kari had created a unique sign for the apostrophe, a quick, fluid motion that somehow conveyed the essence of the punctuation mark. A small detail, but it spoke volumes about Ar'asha's intelligence and adaptability.

Ar'asha's exoskeleton was missing those ridges and spikes that adorned the ambassador's, giving her a more delicate, almost vulnerable look. Was this youth, that would harden as she aged, or was this a part of a spectrum of variation?

The Ren'kari's gentle humming—more like the synths' regular rumbles than the life-support systems'—grew louder as she leaned closer to Mon, now within touching distance. Her sweet, ocean-corn scent wrapped the human in a strange but not unpleasant embrace.

Mon's mind raced with questions, but she forced herself to remain calm, not wanting to overwhelm the young alien. She glanced over her shoulder, wondering what was taking Olve so long to arrive with the communication screens.

As if on cue, Aster's voice cut through the air. "Olve's on his way," they said, their tone a mixture of excitement and apprehension. Aster and Floyd were hanging back, close to the tall keg rack against the wall. Giving them space. "Be here in a minute."

Mon nodded, then turned back to Ar'asha. She raised her hands, signing a simple question. "Why are you here?"

Ar'asha's light patterns flickered, shifting from the steady blue and green to include more agitated purple and orange. She raised another limb, needing two to make the more-complex signs. Her movements slowed and grew less fluid.

"Need... more... green gel... now," Ar'asha signed. With each word, her gestures grew more emphatic.

Mon's brows arched. She turned to Aster and Floyd, whose eyes were almost as wide as Ar'asha's. Aster kept glancing to the side, where the elevators were.

"Did you get that?" she asked them. Both Aster and Floyd shook their heads.

"She wants more green gel. I think she's waiting to take it back with her now. Can we do that?"

Aster nodded. "On it." Both synths hurried back to the refilling room, their footsteps a staccato echo. Moments later, changes in pressure and noise signaled that some new machine had started.

Mon turned back to Ar'asha. "We're getting it now," she signed. Ar'asha's carapace flattened. A sort of sigh? Who really knew.

But if so, why the relief? Didn't the Ren'kari just get a ton of green gel the other day? How could they need more? Had some wedding reception ended up in a drunken orgy?

Before she could form another question to ask, the sound of running human footsteps pounded behind her. Olve burst into the space, one waterproof communication screen in each hand.

In his haste to reach them, he hit the brakes too late. He skidded to a stop, nearly losing his balance on the steeply incline.

The sudden commotion startled Ar'asha. She slipped back into the pool, her light patterns flashing a brilliant red and orange.

Mon's heart sank. Had they just shattered the fragile connection with the young Ren'kari?

Thinking quickly, Mon reached out a hand, palm up, in a gesture she hoped would convey comfort and reassurance. She kept her movements slow and deliberate, not wanting to frighten Ar'asha any further.

To her relief, the Ren'kari's colors slowly shifted back to a more sedate blue and green. Ar'asha cautiously approached the edge of the pool, still under the water, her gaze on Mon's outstretched hand but flicking to Olve, still looming over Mon.

"Sit down," Mon hissed at Olve. She felt him hunch and then hunker into a cross-legged seat just behind her. Now the scent mix included coffee and sweat.

Mon didn't smile at Ar'asha but tried to convey a sense of warmth and understanding. She still wasn't sure where Ren'kari mouths were or how they would interpret a teeth-exposed expression.

She reached her other hand back toward Olve.

"Tablet," she whispered.

He handed it to her. The slippery, shiny tablet. The one the ambassador had used.

Mon brought the hand holding the tablet toward her hand that was waving at Ar'asha. She slowly waved the tablet. Like bait.

Ar'asha hesitated, her limbs twitching, her colors all over the rainbow.

So brave, this little one, to have gotten this far. Would she go further?

With a sudden burst of movement, the Ren'kari propelled herself farther out of the water than before. She reached for the tablet, clamping onto it with all three fingers.

She swished back a bit away from them and perched on the pool's shelf, her longer limbs swaying under the water. Ar'asha set the tablet on the cave floor in front of her. Olve had set the screen to pictographs, but she swiped over to keyboard.

As Ar'asha used two pairs of three digits to type on the device —with impressive speed—Mon exchanged a glance with Olve. If she didn't know GSL, she sure had written Galactic down solid.

His skin gray with exhaustion, still probably hadn't eaten, Olve's eyes were wide, his jaw slack. But his eyes burned bright with eager curiosity.

Together, they watched on the other screen as Ar'asha's words flowed in.

"We know more about human language than we show," Ar'asha wrote, her bioluminescent patterns pulsing in a staccato rhythm, her overtones a steely hum. "Our devices work different, but we can make ours listen to yours."

Olve's breath caught. Mon's mind reeled with the implications.

The Ren'kari had been observing them, studying their technology and language. And yet they had chosen to keep all this knowledge hidden.

Olve's face mirrored her own mixture of excitement and confusion. When they looked back to Ar'asha, she was watching them. Mon nodded and signed, "I understand."

Ar'asha started typing again. "I watch human videos from our receivers above ground. I see your chat groups, but not how to chat."

Mon sucked in a breath and held it. Picturing Ar'asha, this curious maybe young Ren'kari, watching human videos and yearning to communicate. Her giant swirling eyes fixed on a screen trying to absorb the weird mess that is human cultures and languages.

Olve leaned forward, his small brown human eyes locked on the screen, his body thrumming with barely contained excitement. Mon could feel the heat radiating from his skin, almost as warm as the Ren'kari. The intensity of his focus was like a fourth person in the room.

Ar'asha paused, her colors slowing and shifting to a deeper blues and greens and a little red. "I told the Elders I wanted to be an ambassador. But admitting to liking humans has made me an outcast. Not just that, but also..."

Her typing trailed off, leaving a pregnant pause hanging heavy in the humid air.

Wanting to make friends with people your parents didn't want you to. Didn't that feel familiar.

Ar'asha must be here in secret.

Olve, seemingly unable to contain himself any longer, blurted out in GSL, "Then why are you here now?"

Ar'asha froze, her colors shifting to deep reds and orange. The gentle hum in Mon's bones that had accompanied the Ren'kari's presence became fragmented, discordant, painful.

Mon shot Olve a warning glance, silently urging him to tread carefully. His eagerness to learn more about the Ren'kari could override his sense of diplomacy.

Might explain a couple of the hiccups in his long years of research.

She could sense Ar'asha's distress, the way her body language and luminescence betrayed her inner turmoil. She wanted nothing more than to reach out and comfort the young Ren'kari, to assure her that she was safe and accepted here.

But before she could act on that impulse, Ar'asha slipped back into the water, leaving the tablet on the pool deck. Her colors dimmed to a muted gray, then shadow. The chords of her signals—of her self—faded into the background noise of the cave. She was still here, but masking herself, the way the ambassador usually did.

Mon dropped her head toward her lap and sighed.

"What did I say?" Olve whispered, his voice a mixture of frustration and regret.

Mon shook her head, her mind racing as she tried to make sense of Ar'asha's reaction.

"You touched a nerve, is all." She scanned the water, searching for any sign of the young Ren'kari in its shadowy edges.

The soft scrape of metal on stone announced Aster and Floyd's return, each pushing a filled keg. The tart odor of the just-processed gel mingled with the sweet corn of Ar'asha and the brine of the pool, a thick but not unpleasant brew. But the kegs didn't slosh. They thumped.

"What is in those?" Mon said.

"Squeeze pouches," Aster said. "For the gel. It doesn't break down in water, but it's still messy."

Mon stood, hoping that wherever Ar'asha was in the water, she could see her. She signed, "Two kegs are full. Ready. Is that enough?"

Ar'asha's response was immediate. From a swirl of water in the middle of the pool, she was next to the shelf in the time it took Mon to blink. She signed "no" with a sharp, almost violent motion, her colors flashing a bright, urgent maroon. She needed all six kegs filled, and she would bring more soon.

Mon's stomach clenched. Ar'asha's seawater scent had grown sharp and bitter. Mon signed, carefully, using the form that meant the answer was optional, "Why? What happened?"

Ar'asha's limbs twitched and coiled, her agitation palpable. She began to sign, her gestures halting and uncertain, as if she were struggling to find the right words.

Finally, she pulled herself back onto the ledge, her carapace glistening and buzzing with color. She reached for the tablet, her tentacles seeming to shake as she began to type.

"Something has gone wrong, back home." On Olve and Mon's screen, the words pulsed stark and ominous.

"Big talk. Ask humans for help, question. They decide no." She shook the top part of her carapace, the gesture so reminiscent of a human shaking their head that Mon felt a pang of recognition and sympathy.

"But we need the help," Ar'asha continued, her colors shifting to a deep, pulsing blue that seemed to echo the desperation in her words.

Mon's mind raced, trying to piece together the fragments of information into a coherent picture. What could have happened among the Ren'kari that would prompt them to consider asking for human help?

"Is it the green gel?" Olve said. "But they're always getting that."

"Territorial dispute?" Mon said.

Olve shook his head. "We'd have no idea. They never talk about things like that." He grimaced.

Mon stared at Ar'asha, whose attention was now on the next pair of kegs, coming of the filling room. Whatever the problem was, if it was as serious as Ar'asha thought, why had the Ren'kari decided to go it alone?

Chapter Thirteen

Mon pulled her glacier-cold feet out of the cargo cave pool and knelt beside its edge. Even the chill of the air burned her toes. The boots might be a total loss.

Small price to pay for such a breakthrough.

The Ren'kari knew how to speak Galactic!

Well, type it.

Ar'asha's slender limbs danced across the communications tablet's screen. The little Ren'kari's bioluminescence pulsed in a becoming-familiar pattern of blue and green, casting the softest jewel shadows on the damp stone edge of the moon pool.

Olve must have gone to check on the kegs. It would be only a few more minutes before the other four were filled. Once she had her kegs, Ar'asha would surely bolt.

But for now she was typing, fast and steady. As if her life depended on it.

"The key is in the sound," Ar'asha typed, her movements swift and precise. "Each phrase, each word, is accompanied by a specific sound. Vibration? It carries meaning beyond the gestures or light-words."

Mon's eyes widened as she tried to understand. Could this be the elusive piece of the puzzle that had been tormenting Olve for so long? More likely only one of the pieces.

But a piece.

"Show me, please" she signed.

Ar'asha made the signs for "See you tomorrow," accompanied by a pleasant keening tone that was almost within human hearing.

"Means glad," she typed.

She made the signs again, this time with a dissonant chord far lower than standard human, but well within Listener range.

"Means get ready for a fight."

Mon touched her pocket, where her Listening device was on, recording. She ached to grab it and see if that distinction made it onto the recording, but she was too soggy to dare try. Instead, she turned to ask how much Olve could take in of this revelation.

But the words died on her tongue as she realized he was nowhere to be seen.

Blasted comets.

A sinking feeling settled in Mon's stomach as she scanned the open space. He wasn't by the tools and tables, nor the wetsuits. Maybe the gel vat room? Seemed unlikely.

Or had he, in a fit of pique and frustration, stomped out of the room altogether?

Surely she would have heard that. But her mind and senses had been focused on the Ren'kari. The other turtle sea rover could've come back, and Mon might not have noticed.

But this. This might be a problem.

Ar'asha seemed to sense Mon's unease, her bioluminescence dimming to muted blues and greens. She tilted her head, her now-multicolored eyes reflecting the soft light of the cave as she studied Mon's face.

"Something wrong?" Ar'asha signed, her movements slower, almost hesitant.

Mon forced a close-lipped smile, shaking her head. "It's nothing," she signed, her motions looking hollow even to her own eyes.

She turned her attention back to the tablet, trying to focus on the breakthrough they had just made. How could she make it clear to non-Listeners? But the nagging sense of worry continued to gnaw at her. Unnecessary worry. Olve would never do anything to impede progress.

Not his own progress, obviously. But what about someone else's?

As if sensing her distress, Ar'asha reached out a tentative limb, the tips of her three fingers brushing against Mon's arm in a gesture that was both alien and strangely comforting. The Ren'kari's touch was warm and softly rough, like the surface of a heated brick. Mon found herself leaning into the contact.

Metal on stone. Aster and Floyd pushed the last of the kegs to the edge of the pool. All six were ready. Now the burnt summer grass smell of the green gel overpowered even the brine in the air.

Floyd wrapped a thick length of cord around each keg. Once the train was complete, she handed the end of the cord to Ar'asha.

"Ready," Floyd signed.

Ar'asha took the cord, careful not to touch Floyd's hand, and rocketed herself backward into the water. Like fat dominoes, each keg tipped into the pool, one after the other.

When they were all in and already sinking, Ar'asha popped her carapace and two limbs out of the water.

"See you tomorrow," she signed, accompanied by that high, happy keen. Her bioluminescence flickered blues, reds, and oranges as she disappeared beneath the surface of the water.

As the pool's natural movement erased the ripples left in Ar'asha's wake, Mon's mind ran through the implications of their breakthrough. To understand the emotions—the feelings—behind the language! She had to get the Listening device's data online right now and use it figure a way for everyone else to read the signals.

She needed to find Olve, and get one of those black boxes to fill with Listener data. And she should listen through all the other recordings, the earlier ones. Maybe overtones were being recorded all the time and no one could hear them?

Then she felt something else. Something strong, and familiar.

The Ren'kari ambassador was here. Up, at the lab.

She lurched to her feet, wincing as her frozen toes protested the sudden movement. The ambassador must have come from above. Mon hadn't heard their approach down here.

"What is it?" Aster said.

"Ambassador's here," she said, stumbling toward the elevators at the back of the cave. Aster passed her and held the elevator door open, and they rode up together.

All down the long hall to the lab, Mon must have been hearing the normal hums, screeches, and clicks of the base. But she only had Listener ears for the ambassador.

Their overtones were thicker. Angrier? As Aster and Mon drew closer to the lab, Mon panting with the exertion, she started to slow. Something was wrong; she could feel it in the way the hairs on the back of her neck stood on end, in the way the sound-senses rocked and crashed into her.

Aster reached the lab and pushed the button to slide it open. Mon rolled in right behind them, her breaths thick as she took in the scene before her.

Olve stood at the large observation windows, his body tense as he faced the Ren'kari ambassador, floating just as tense beyond the glass.

The ambassador's crystalline exoskeleton glinted in the ocean's dim afternoon light, their bioluminescence pulsing in jagged swirls of reds and oranges. Even through the barrier of the window, Mon could feel the weight of their presence, the power and authority.

"What are you doing?" Mon demanded, her voice cutting through the quiet murmur of the lab equipment.

Olve turned to face her, his expression a mix of frustration and triumph.

"I sent an emergency signal to the ambassador," he said. "To discuss our little surprise visitor." He paused, as if he couldn't think of another reason. "And to ask about the sudden increase in demand for the green gel."

Mon's stomach clenched as she realized the depth of Olve's betrayal. He had gone behind Ar'asha's back, risking their already fragile relationship with the Ren'kari in his quest for...what? Control? Surely not answers. Not the way he was acting now.

The ambassador's eyes somehow narrowed, their multifaceted surface reflecting the cold light of the lab.

"Is it true?" they asked, their signs chopping, their silent chord sounding in Mon's bones a low growl. "Have you been communicating with the inferior, Ar'asha?"

Mon stepped forward, meeting the ambassador's gaze head-on. "Yes," she signed. "Ar'asha"—at the finger spelling the ambassador's colors blinked orange—"came to us, willing to bridge the gap between our peoples."

Olve stepped in front of her.

"Don't bring politics into it," he hissed.

The ambassador's colors pulsed in a discordant rhythm, their agitation palpable.

"You do not understand," they signed. "This one is not just an inferior among our people. She is... different."

Olve, only now seeming to sense the opportunity in all this chaos, leaned forward, his face a mask of eager curiosity.

"Different how?" he asked, his signs low and close to his chest, conspiratorial.

The ambassador hesitated, their crystalline shell blinking slow. For a moment, Mon thought they might refuse to answer, but then they spoke, their words heavy with a weight that seemed to press down on the very air itself.

"Ar'asha is an anomaly," they signed, their luminescence dimming. "Her very existence challenges the fundamental beliefs of our society, the carefully cultivated harmony that has sustained us for generations."

Her very existence? She looked like all the others Mon had seen in pictures and in person. Maybe she was a little more gray, but so was the ambassador at the moment. What could be so different about Ar'asha that it would threaten the very fabric of Ren'kari society?

"I don't understand," Olve signed.

The ambassador curtly signed, "No."

Olve, frustrated, jumped to a new subject. "And what about the green gel?" he asked, his signs tight with frustration. "Why the sudden increase in demand?"

The ambassador's eyes flashed, a surging display of reds and oranges.

"That is a matter for the Ren'kari," they signed. "It is the inferior's role to transport the kegs. That is all. No more communication. Yes?"

Without hesitation, Olve nodded. "Yes," he signed.

Mon's heart sank as she watched the exchange. How could Olve give up the chance to get the knowledge he'd spent more than a decade trying to find? Was he that jealous? But Ar'asha had communicated with both of them, not just Mon.

Whatever it was—envy, exhaustion, panic—Olve had stomped on the delicate threads of their relationship with the Ren'kari. This argument could be catastrophic for both their peoples.

The ambassador began to drift away backwards from the window. "We will discuss these matters further amongst our people," they signed, starting to fade into the shadows. "And then we will decide whether to continue our communication with your kind."

Olve gasped. "Wait!" he signed.

But the ambassador was gone.

Mon clomped to the window, her wet feet still frozen. She turned to Olve, her eyes burning with a mixture of anger and disbelief.

"Do you realize what you've done?" she said.

Olve held her gaze, his jaw clenched tight.

"I did what I had to do," he said, his tone defensive and unyielding. "Theirs is a hierarchical society. We couldn't be seen going around the ambassador's back. We have to keep the main line of communication open."

But his face had gone from sickly gray to white.

Mon snorted. After all they'd learned of the Ren'kari. The people who knew far more about humans than humans did about them.

"Bravo," she said.

Chapter Fourteen

The Ren'kari ambassador left a noisy silence in their wake.

Mon glared out the large observation windows, her gaze following a family of lanternfish as she tried to get her emotions in check. The tension in the lab was a storm cloud ready to loose thunder on all their heads.

Or maybe that was just the tension in her head.

Beside her, not looking at her, Olve was a coiled spring. His hands gripped the vertical supports of one of windows, his knuckles white.

Aster stood at another window few steps away, as if afraid to get too close. Their face, usually so bright, tipped into a frown as they watched the two humans.

The click-whirr-screes of the lab's machinery could not fill the silence. The pressure of it pressed down on Mon. The responsibility of bridging the gap between their two species.

She spun away from the window, to face Olve. Her eyes narrowed as she took in his rigid posture.

"We need to talk about what just happened," she said.

Olve's head snapped to her face, his hair flying, eyes blazing with manic intensity.

"What's there to talk about?" he snarled, his voice ragged. "You went behind my back and talked to another Ren'kari. Twice. You undermined everything I've been working towards."

Mon let the anger flare, her hands clenching into fists at her sides, and then released it. She took a breath. Scents of salt and hot metal and this morning's sweet pastry filled her lungs, grounding her in the moment.

"I did not go behind your back," she said, her voice measured and even. "Ar'asha came to us. All of us. You were there. She wants to help."

Olve scoffed, his lips twisting into a sneer. "A child. She doesn't know anything about anything. The ambassador is the only one who matters."

Aster stepped forward, their hands held out in a placating gesture. They smelled of vinegar, or whatever it was that they made the gel with. Mon hadn't even noticed when she was stumbling down the hall to get to the lab.

"Olve," Aster said, their voice soft and soothing. "I know you're frustrated, but we need to think this through. Ar'asha could be a valuable asset."

Olve rounded on Aster so fast his arms had to check his sway.

"You're taking her side?" he said, voice cracking. "After everything we've been through?"

Aster flinched. "I'm not taking anyone's side," they said, their voice steady despite the hurt in their eyes. "I'm just looking for a way forward."

"They're going to kick us off this planet!" Olve said. "We have to follow their rules."

"We are following their rules!" Aster shot back. "We did not initiate that contact. We did not invade their space, even if their space is the entire ocean. Practically."

The tension in the room seemed to ratchet up with every word. The buzzy air crackled with the force of Olve's rage.

She took a half-step forward, her hands held out in a gesture of peace.

"Olve," she said, her voice soft and hopefully coaxing. "I can see why you're upset. But think. We can't afford to give up on Ar'asha. She's our key to understanding the Ren'kari. It's obvious that the others don't want to help us."

Aster nodded. "And they know all about us," they said. "The ambassadors could have been helping us all this time. And not one of them has."

Olve shook his head. His mouth twisted so tightly that Mon winced.

Aster gestured at the big meeting table. The black boxes were still there, but all the floating screens had been shut off.

"How about we have a seat and talk about it?" they said.

Olve turned away, back toward the window. Not looking at them.

"You don't understand," he said, grabbing his elbows, pulling his arms into his body. "I've spent years trying to crack this language. Earning their trust so they will speak with us. With me. To keep us all safe."

The man was all over the place. Mon couldn't keep up.

Aster moved to stand beside Olve, their hand coming to rest on his shoulder. Olve flinched at the contact. His body looked so rigid a hard blow might crack him in half.

"Olve," Aster said. "This isn't about you. You know that. It's about understanding. We need to work together, not against each other. The same way we always have."

Olve wrenched himself away from Aster's touch, his eyes hard.

"Work together?" he said. "Like you worked together with her to go behind my back?"

Mon threw up her hands in disgust.

"You'll never get through to him, Aster," she said. "Give it up."

"No!" Aster reached for Olve again. "We have to work together. We do. None of us can solve this on our own."

But Olve wasn't listening. He pushed against the glass to turn away from Aster. Olve's shoulders hunched even more. His fists clenched against his upper thighs. He paced across the lab, his footsteps slapping the soft black flooring.

Aster shook their head. They looked at Mon, eyes sad.

"It's not your fault," they said. "Olve is just... he's been under a lot of pressure lately."

"So have we all," said Mon.

"I can hear you both," Olve said.

"Then grow up and work with us," Mon said.

Aster groaned.

Olve stopped pacing. He turned to stare at Mon, and then at Aster. His face wasn't filled with anger anymore. It was blank.

"Going to the gym," he said. "Work off a little... pressure."

He stomped out of the lab.

As the door slid shut after him, Aster dropped into one of the padded chairs at the big meeting table.

"Well, that could have gone better," they said.

Mon had no time for commiseration. Let Aster solve this problem. They were the lab manager, after all.

She went to the black box that stored the audio and video clips, and settled in the chair in front of it. She opened a screen and started rolling the clips at double speed.

She'd solve this problem by herself, if she had to.

"Find me a big space on one of these boxes, would you," she said. "I need to dump today's recordings."

Aster didn't move. They covered their eyes with a top hand. "We need to find a way to reach Olve, to show him that we're on his side."

"Sounds like we don't want to be on his side," Mon said. "He is turning down valuable information for the promise of fool's gold."

"I don't know that phrase," Aster said. "Oh, I see. Yes. Quite appropriate."

Mon stared at the screen, her mind trying to parse the images of Ren'kari behavior, match them to the patterns of light, reach for any patterns outside sound.

The actions and sounds from previous encounters played out before her, but she could not seem to focus. Something else was on her mind.

She turned to Aster, who was still just sitting at the meeting table. Moping.

"Something has changed," Mon said. "Besides the thing with Ar'asha, I mean."

Aster tilted their head, gazing at her, eyes bleak.

"The Ren'kari didn't seem to need to trade with the earlier humans, but now they're demanding it," she said. "And while the ambassador is belittling us, they aren't stopping their demands for help."

Aster's eyebrows lifted. Their head snapped up. They frowned.

"You're right," they said. "It's certainly a shift in their behavior."

Aster spun in their chair, their gaze drifting to the observation windows. The olive blue of the afternoon undersea seemed to hold no answers.

"Could be anything," they said. "A change in their environment. A shift in their political structure. Something we would never even have considered."

Mon turned back to the screen, her fingers hovering over the controls. There were thousands—tens of thousands—of video and audio files in this black box.

"We have to keep digging," she said.

Aster pushed both sets of their hands together in a prayer position.

"I'm going to go into the files in the most direct way," they said. "It will look like I'm meditating."

It did. In the now-low hum of the lab, Mon turned her attention back to the screen. She trained her mind onto the task at hand and opened her Listener senses wide. She let the media files flow. Let the sounds, lights, and movement of the Ren'kari fill her mind.

The complex harmonies and discordant tones wash over her. Somewhere in this chaos of sensation, there had to be an answer.

And she would find it.

Chapter Fifteen

Alone in the ocean-view lab the next morning, Mon scratched the skin under one of her emergency rebreather's backpack straps. She could almost forget she was always wearing the thing, except for that one itch just over her right collarbone.

Luckily, the padded chairs around the long meeting table easily accommodated turtle-backed humans. The back and seat looked firm, but when you warmed them up, they started to mold themselves to your back and butt. Or in Mon's case, her whole leg.

She sat cross-legged, wrapped in her new sweater, staring at a pair of screens. The same ones she'd been staring at—Listening to—last night when her eyelids began to droop. The ones with the sounds that haunted her dreams.

Whispers of Ren'kari overtones that weren't really there. She'd lurch up in bed, thinking a Ren'kari was coming. As soon as she was awake, the sense would fade.

Overnight, the temperature in the lab had dropped. With only the two black processing boxes that she needed in use, it wouldn't warm up that much. She wrapped her sweater tighter around her.

Mon had left the overhead lights off, using only the small display lights on the shelves that held the artifacts for light. The water outside was lightening from gray-black to olive, adding the slightest bit more light. But really, she was just staring at these screens or had her eyes closed, Listening, how much light did she need?

Olve had not returned to the lab last night. Aster said Olve had run himself ragged on the rowing machine. Then he actually willingly ate a protein bar and closed himself up in his room. No one had seen him since.

Whatever.

Except, blast it all to bits, she needed him.

She needed someone else to listen. To confirm.

To celebrate.

Mon had spent the last eight hours of yesterday running through decades' worth of recordings. Listening. Straining to hear the Ren'kari overtones that Ar'asha had shown her were there.

Joke was on Mon, though.

When she finally did hear some tones—in recordings from a decade ago when the researchers were testing different ranges of light—the signal was so loud she flinched as if she'd been slapped. The noise-canceling 'phones were no help, and neither was the sound controls. These not-sounds did not respond to the volume slider.

After that, she quickly found several sections of recordings from the past that contained the happy overtones. And many, many, that sounded much less agreeable.

The Ren'kari were screechers. Like space station gravity thrusters, only using shorter blasts.

It looked like light was the main communication method, with sound—including Listener sounds—supplying the emotional valence and tenses. Chemical signals did not show any language-like patterns. Maybe they acted subconsciously, like pheromones in humans?

The breakthrough felt better than even the apple pancakes Aster had made for everyone this morning.

Where was Aster? Probably rustling up some more green-gel powder. The elevators had sung their up and down song all night, bringing in supplies, trying to catch up to Ren'kari demand.

Mon sorted the recordings with target sounds into groups based on what she thought the conversation was about. Mostly when and where questions, and discussions of amount and volume.

The conversations from Olve's point of view looked the same. The arm motions and the patterns of bioluminescence were pretty regular.

But the overtones told a different story. The lights could say yes, now, while the overtones said not really, never.

The "happy" overtones, like the ones Ar'asha had made yesterday—sat tantalizingly close to normal human range. The others—the majority of them—didn't register on her ears. They seemed to take some other conduit directly to her mind.

But these happy ones—surely Olve could hear these? If he knew what to listen for.

She packaged a good collection of the happy clips and wrote a quick report. She sent it to Olve and to Aster the slow way, but pinged them on her new comms interface to say it was coming.

Watching these clips of Olve was a revelation. The skinny, spotty brown boy from twenty years ago, face alight, visibly vibrating with excitement, had slowly morphed into a lanky, stern, ashy man whose emotions seemed to have leached away. All that remained was anger.

No wonder the Ren'kari ambassador held him at arm's length.

Or had that been the ambassador's plan all along?

Over the years, the bulk of the Ren'kari's tones had grown more... strident? Angry? Belittling? She didn't know enough yet to be sure. But Olve must have had some sense of it, to respond to it as he had.

And just as it was the same human, it was the same Ren'kari in these recordings, down all these years.

Who knew how long Ren'kari lived? Aster said they weren't sure, but that this Ren'kari had more than once referred to the earlier humans as if they knew them. The humans they'd killed.

If that was true, maybe the rudeness was the plan. Wear down the single pushy human until he gave up so they could go back to rotating contacts. Return to keeping the humans at sea's length.

Poor Olve.

No response to her messages yet. Mon pulled up all the Listening device data from Ar'asha's visit on her second screen, scanning all the spectra the device's app offered.

How did Heather tease out a single signal from all of these readings? Mon just ran the whole gamut, looking for patterns and similarities.

The device had also recorded Aster and Floyd. The signals confirmed Mon's hypothesis that each synth had a Listener pattern, too. But the synths' readings needed to be magnified to read true, while the Ren'kari needed to be turned way down.

This discovery was incredible. She looked to the door, trying to will someone to come in so she could share her excitement.

Still no response to her message.

Aster should have had something to say, some quip.

Olve should be here.

She had to talk to someone. Right now.

Mon pinged Heather. Okay to talk now?

Yes! pinged back immediately.

"Guess what?" Heather said the moment the voice connection

opened. Her words echoed as if she were in a big hall. "We set a record clearing Apple Island! Just tons of apples, everywhere. We left two of the big floater container things at your base. We'll pick them up as soon as everybody is settled. But take as many as you want. One floater can feed a town for a year."

"It's nice to hear from you, too," Mon said, laughing. She heard a door slam on Heather's link and the background grew quieter.

"So, listen." Heather said. "If I volunteer to go back for the floaters, can you get me down to the base? I heard it was supercool, right?"

Mon groaned.

"Just for an hour or two," Heather said. "Not so long I'd need to depressurize or anything."

"I'd love it if you did, but it's not a good time. I'm trying to get the research chief to invite you, but right now I'm on his shit list."

"What, you did something better than him?"

The hall door slid open. Olve came in at a lope, half of a folded pancake in one hand. His hair was a mess but his skin tone was healthier. He must have slept. He beelined for the workstation at the near end of the meeting table, his usual spot, and fired up its screens.

"Sorry," Mon said to Heather. "But I do want to tell you your Listening device works great down here. And we made a break-through!"

"I already know all about that," Heather said. "Floyd runs one of the chatrooms I like, and she told me."

Well, that was a bit deflating. Thanks, Floyd.

"Well, not all," Heather continued. "Floyd couldn't give me the details, and she says you can't either. Top secret! Stupid politics. It's a new language, right? Floyd says she might be able to get me on-base as her mentee. Next rotation. How about that?"

"Listen," Mon said to Heather. "Can you hear the synthetic humans around you? I'm getting readings on the people down here with us, but I don't have enough experience to know whether that's normal or not."

The door opened again, this time, Aster. They joined Olve at his station, leaning over his chair to look at the screens. They looked fresh and rested, and smelled of cut grass and apple preserves.

"Yes," Heather said. "But it's soft-soft-soft. Not like machines. Or space crap."

Olve started playing the clips Mon had sent. He closed his eyes. Aster crossed both sets of arms, face going still. Both listening intently.

"Can you tell each person apart?" Mon asked Heather, trying to ignore the screeches and rumbles from the clips.

"Huh," Heather said. "Maybe? They're whispers, synth sounds, I just block them. Kinda like invasion of privacy not to. I guess?"

Mon was losing focus. She shook her head, trying to dislodge the sudden pain from her mind. Olve was playing the sample clips at a low level, but even so the screaming overtones gouged Mon's nerves.

She had to get out of here.

She unfolded from the chair, starting to stand.

And staggered, almost falling into Olve's setup. Stupid foot was asleep again. High pressure wrecked a body's grace.

Mon could not hear herself think. She glared at Olve.

"Put on some earphones, would you?" she said.

Olve, startled, put the clip on pause. The screaming disappeared.

Blessed relative silence.

Aster took off for Olve's workstation-castle at the other end of the room and started rummaging around.

"Wait!" Heather said on the phone. "What was that sound?"

Mon couldn't believe it.

"You heard that? On this crap connection?"

"Was hecka loud, hello," Heather said. "Play it again?"

Mon sighed. She looked at Olve, whose eyes were wide, mouth slightly open. As if he'd never had anybody yell at him before.

"Let it play," she said to him. To Heather, she said, "I'm going to put you on speaker. See what you think."

As the tones started up again, Mon clenched her jaw, grabbed her elbows in her hands, tried to set her mental blocks higher, struggled to tamp down the screeching.

"Why are they screaming?" Heather asked aloud on the speaker.

"They're big," said Olve.

"Guess so. You're Olve, right?" Heather wasted no time. "Can you send me those files? It would be faster for me to calibrate my reader than to teach Mon how to do it."

Olve looked at Mon. Mon shrugged.

"It would," Mon said. "Heather's the pro. She designed the thing."

Olve frowned.

The recordings continued to screech.

"If it's easier," Heather said, "slide 'em up on the tech chat boards. Even if no one else can sense them, they can confirm the signal once we point to where it is."

"Great idea," Mon said. She really had to get on those chat boards.

"Yeah," Heather said. "I'm the best."

Olve ran a hand through his hair, snagging on a tangle somewhere near his ear. Apple preserves, probably. He grimaced.

"We put it on the chats and everyone will know," he said.

"Ugh," Heather said.

Mon had not missed the girl's full-bellied groan at all. Olve scowled.

"Everybody who?" Heather said. "Listen, there's only three people on this whole stupid planet who aren't permanent residents of Arkhide, right? One already knows your secret, one has guessed. The other one has her nose so deep in space-time equations she forgot she was supposed to have dinner with me last week."

Aster came back to the table holding the two raggediest headphones Mon had seen since wartime. Olve waved them away.

"What do you think you know, young lady?" Olve said.

Now Mon groaned. Seriously? Young lady? Aster slapped their hand to their forehead, apparently forgetting the headphones they were holding, which punched them in the nose.

"Let me see," Heather said, dangerously sweetly. "Something near your base is sending silicon signatures so strong they scream. Something that varies its signatures, not like a machine would do. Hmmm. Wonder if the Cooperative Realm knows there's another species living on Arkhide?"

Aster and Olve shared a look of panic.

Mon reached over and put the sounds on pause again.

"Lucky guess," Olve muttered.

"Brilliant, nearly adult, lady," Heather said on the speaker.

"She has really good hearing," Mon said to Aster. "I mean, we do."

Olve twined his fingers together and grabbed the back of his neck. "Okay, fine," he said. "Then what?"

"Then what, what?" Aster said.

Mon jumped in before Heather could rattle on. Before Olve could get his mouth around "No."

"Then, Heather can describe the spectrum, in math," Mon said. "We figure how to block the signal."

And something else.

"And then," she looked at Olve, "we tune our other devices to receive and send them."

She flicked her gaze to Aster. "And maybe even the synthetic humans."

Aster's face lit up, as if she'd offered him a gift.

Olve wasn't scowling. He tapped a small scar on his temple.

"And the humans with implants, too."

He pulled his hands up off his neck and dragged them through his hair. He dragged his hands down his face.

"Silicon," he said. He stared at the screen showing the near-spectrum image of the clip he had been playing. The sound waves spiked off the top of the screen.

They needed to recalibrate the charts.

Mon could hear the overtones, even on pause.

No. these were real. Different from the pattern on-screen, but still familiar. Coming from the left.

"What is that?" Heather said just as Mon identified the sound-signature.

"Ren'kari ambassador," she said. "Gotta go."

And Ar'asha. Coming from below.

Chapter Sixteen

As if they were a synchronized swim team, Mon, Aster, and Olve turned to the lab's ocean-view windows and looked to the left. The direction the Ren'kari ambassador came from.

Olve pushed his chair away from the oval meeting table and got to his feet. Aster was closest to the observation windows, but Olve got there first.

"Wonder what they're going to lie to us about today," he said.

Mon grabbed her blocker headphones before heading to the window. Slipping them on cast the hum of the lab's machinery and the whirrs and whooshes of the base's life support systems into deep background in her mind. She needed all the space she could get for the complex soundings of this Ren'kari.

The soft glow of the screens behind her cast an eerie orange light across the lab, mingling with the muted white-yellow from the shelves holding the artifacts. But all eyes were on the ocean outside the windows, its green-brown murk signaling late afternoon.

Mon, farthest away, was the last to reach the window, standing to Aster's right. Olve stood on the other side. Tension radiated off them, in the stiffness of Olve's back, in the clasping of both sets of Aster's arms. Frustration, desperation and a sense of what the heck now?

Mon heard the ambassador's signal change, like before. A moment later, a flicker of movement caught her eye, and she turned to see the Ren'kari ambassador emerging from the depths. Their bioluminescent patterns pulsed in the calm range. But as they approached the window, Mon's Listener senses picked up on something off in their usual sound-signature, a discordant note.

The ambassador settled into their usual position, facing the window, exoskeleton behind, their legs and most of their arms floating gracefully beneath them. Olve turned to Aster and gestured towards the dive room.

"Get the comms tablets?" Aster nodded and hurried off, their footsteps soft against the dark flooring.

But before they could return, the ambassador raised an arm and pointed at Mon. Their body flashed in a new pattern, reds and oranges and dark purple.

"The bushy-head one must leave," they signed. "We will not speak with it."

Harsh. Mon fought the urge to reach up and pat down her hair. Not her fault it was so humid down here. She glanced at Olve, searching his face for any sign of support or protest. She found only a mix of surprise and resignation.

"Did it to yourself," Olve muttered.

So that's how it was.

Aster, busy placing the ambassador's tablet into the airlock and filling the lock with water, had not seen the interaction.

Mon forced herself to take a deep breath, the tang of salt and metal filling her lungs. Fine. She would leave.

But not completely.

She pivoted, passing the angle to the hallway door and stopping at the table. A few quick steps, and she'd grabbed the Listening device. She clicked it to record and set it back on the table.

With a final glance at Olve and the ambassador, Mon turned and walked towards the door. She could feel their gazes burning into her back.

Joke was on them.

Mon didn't stop walking as the door slid shut behind her. What was wrong with the ambassador? The discordant notes of their sound-signature remained, even without Mon to trigger them.

And why was Ar'asha around here, but not with the ambassador? Was she in trouble? Surely she also had been told to stay away from the humans.

Mon tapped her network feed and pinged Floyd, down in the cargo cave. The engineer's icon—a cute pink panda—flashed on her wristcom as the call connected.

"Seen Ar'asha around?" Mon asked. She had to swallow, throat tight with leftover bitterness at the ambassador's slight.

"Yeah," Floyd said. "Was about to ping you. Think she's asking for you. Keeps finger-spelling a name with three letters. Least, I think it's a name."

"On my way," she said, quickening her pace as she made her way towards the elevators.

Should she tell Olve?

Mon paused at the elevator, her finger hovering over the call button. If she told Olve or Aster, they could help her ask the right questions of Ar'asha—and understand her answers. But what if it lead to more conflict with the ambassador? If she kept mum and they found out, that might shatter the trust they were building.

But what about just holding off a bit?

The elevator dinged, and Mon stepped inside, her reflection

staring back at her from the lemon-polished metal walls. Honesty and transparency? Secrecy and discretion? She leaned against the wall, taking in its familiar grinding burr, her mind racing. She wouldn't risk putting Ar'asha in any danger.

Any more danger.

Was Mon even qualified to make this call? What if she was wrong, and it all blew up in her face? The thought of being responsible for damaging the fragile alliance they had worked so hard for—or further damaging it, from Olve's point of view—made Mon's stomach churn.

The elevator slowed to a stop. Treat it like a mission. Focus on the goal—clear communication.

Mon straightened her spine. Gathering intel was the priority. She could decide what to do with it after—if—she actually had any.

The doors slid open, revealing an even pinker than usual Floyd. She had swapped her hands for four-pronged pincers, painted light coral.

"Kid brought more empty squeeze bags for the gel," Floyd said, her voice so low it barely echoed in the cavernous space. "Think she's waiting for refills. Gonna take a while. Twins and I are working fast as we can"—she held up her hands, touching the pincers together, clearly more precise than puffy fingers would be —"but takes a little time."

Mon nodded, and looked past Floyd. Ar'asha perched on the step just below the pool's edge, the bioluminescent patterns on her arms pulsing. Her carapace and other segments of her exoskeleton also pulsed, dimmer through the gray of her shell compared to the transparency of the ambassador's shell. Mon's eyes traced the curve of the young Ren'kari's back. Why such a difference?

The turtle-shaped sea rover was still moored to the far side of the pool, bright white in the white-bluish light of the cave. But now it had a mate, behind it on the recharge platform. Must be the rover the other synthetic humans had been piloting before.

The gentle lapping of the water against the pool's near edge mingled with the nearby hum of the gel processing machinery. Everything else was still muted by her headphones.

Everything but Ar'asha.

"She's been asking for the tablet," said Floyd said while matching Mon's steps toward the pool. "Glad I remembered the sign for it."

She handed Mon the other of the paired tablets. Its smooth metal chilled her palm. The cave wasn't cold, but it wasn't warm, either.

A pang of guilt washed over Mon. They needed these tablets upstairs, for the ambassador. Would she have to rip it out of her little friends sharp-tipped fingers?

Check first. She pinged Aster, text only. *Need the comms tablets? They're in the cargo cave.*

Got spares up here, Aster texted back. A pause, and then, *Ar'asha?*

So much for all that worrying about secrecy.

Yes.

Don't tell Olve. I'll handle it.

Mon stared at the screen until the message blinked out.

Aster, an ally. Who knew?

Synthetic humans were turning out to be okay, despite their perfect features and superhuman strength. Aster's cheer, Floyd's quick thinking. Even Aimee Five's singleminded purpose, so like Olve's and yet so much less shrill. Mon breathed in the scent of saltwater and metal and dusty rose that clung to the Floyd's skin, finding comfort in the familiarity of it all.

This time, Mon discarded her boots and socks on the cave floor before taking the last steps to the pool. The rough stone of the pool's edge chilled her bare feet, a stark contrast to the warmth emanating from the young Ren'kari.

Settling cross-legged a little to the side of Ar'asha, who was already busily typing with the fingers of two of her arms, Mon drank in the sight of her.

The intricacy of her carapace and segments, the speed and grace of her movements. The scent of the ocean clung to Ar'asha's skin, mingling with a faint, sweet corn aroma that Mon couldn't quite believe. Beneath it all, the steady thrum of the kid's unique sound-signature washed through Mon's mind.

Another of Ar'asha's arms broke the surface of the water. It reached up to tap Mon gently on the knee. Mon startled, her eyes meeting the young Ren'kari's gaze. Ar'asha's large oval eyes swirled silver and every other color, deep and fathomless.

With a quick, almost impatient gesture, Ar'asha tap-tapped Mon's knee again, and then tapped the tablet in Mon's hand.

Look at the tablet.

Right. Mon nodded. She clicked the screen on as she heard Floyd heading back to the production room. She turned to the synthetic human.

"Floyd? Could you stay?"

Floyd turned back, confusion in the tilt of her eyebrows.

"I need a second pair of eyes? I don't have the recorder, and I want to catch everything."

The smile that spread across Floyd's face was so wide it looked like it might crack her cheeks. She held up a single finger—wait—and sped up to the entrance to the production room. A quick check with someone in the room, and Floyd nodded and made her way back down. She squatted slightly behind Mon.

"Don't want to loom over everybody," she said.

Mon held the screen so they both could read it. Ar'asha's words, black marks on white, filled the display.

"Our people are sick," the message began, the stark words seeming to pulse with the same intensity as Ar'asha's bioluminescent patterns. "The tectonic shift that devastated your land above also destroyed our cave holding our reserves. This gel is vital to keep our shells sturdy and our bodies safe."

The degeneration had been gradual, Ar'asha wrote. Ren'kari lived for centuries, but changes in their society over time made it more important to stay below than go above. In the old days, she said, most Ren'kari would go up-top for a few months every ten or twenty years. Sort of like a working vacation. They would harvest the powder, apply it to themselves and let it bake in, and then bring it in gel form back down for the people who couldn't spare the time or energy to go up themselves.

They didn't realize they had a problem until the Time of the First Humans. When their strongest fighters returned from decimating the human settlers, they were weak. Parts of their shells had disintegrated. The sun had damaged their skeletons.

This had never happened before.

The few Ren'kari who could still withstand the pressures of being up-top would harvest as much nutrient as they could, working at night and doing as much of the processing as possible under water.

That's why, a century later, when the New Humans came, and asked politely to stay, the Ren'kari let them live.

"When you came," Ar'asha typed, "and tried to follow our rules, we knew we could make a deal."

"Bamboo," Floyd whispered. "That's all this powder is. Silica leached from bamboo. How could it be key to their survival?"

Mon nodded but didn't answer. Her mind was full, racing to follow the path of Ar'asha's revelation. Aster had told Mon that the green gel was important to the Ren'kari. But no one had said anything about life or death.

Ar'asha watched them, her huge oval eyes whirring. Mon finished reading and looked up at her.

"How serious is this problem?" Mon signed.

Ar'asha's response was immediate and visceral. One of her arms snaked out of the water, wrapping around Mon's forearm with a surprising strength. Mon gasped as the young Ren'kari tugged her close, the sticky warmth of her arm a shock against Mon's bare skin.

"Careful!" Floyd said, grabbing Mon's shoulder as she scrambled to her knees to regain her balance. "Don't wing the kid."

With a gentle insistence, Ar'asha guided Mon's hand to the surface of her shell, inviting her to feel the texture for herself. Mon's fingers trembled, but nothing happened as they hovered above the shell. Nothhing as she lightly touched the surface. No poison, no shock, no sting.

Mon traced the intricate patterns of Ar'asha's skeleton, so supple. Like touching a piece of fine silk over soft bone, delicate and fragile. Nothing like the tough, unyielding armor she had expected.

Floyd's grip on Mon's shoulder tightened, her pincers digging into the fabric of Mon's shirt.

"Whatsit feel like?" she breathed.

"Soft," Mon said. "Like the skin of a ripe peach, or the petals of a flower. But there's texture to it, too, like the ridges on a seashell."

"Or bamboo," Floyd said.

The colors playing across the surface of Ar'asha's exoskeleton shifted and swirled in response to Mon's hand. It was like touching a living kaleidoscope.

"It should be strong," Ar'asha signed. "Like rock."

Reluctantly, Mon pulled away. She needed both hands to sign.

"How to help?" Mon signed. There must be something more lasting than using some gel year after year.

Ar'asha unslung her arm from Mon's.

"Don't know," she said, her signs slow and deliberate. She went back to the tablet and started typing. "You must treat the ambassador with respect. Our people are proud."

The ambassador was a puffed-up peacock. But Mon would do what she had to do.

Floyd's pincers were still resting on her shoulder, a comforting weight at the moment.

Mon pointed to Floyd and spoke out loud as well as signing.

"This is Floyd. Can she touch you, too? She is clever with tools."

Behind her, Floyd gasped.

"Please please please please please," she whispered.

Ar'asha's arm snaked out again, this time for Floyd's arm. The pink synth quickly scooted around Mon, trying to keep her arm in its socket as the Ren'kari tugged. Floyd was careful to touch the same areas as Mon had.

Ar'asha's colors exploded again.

Floyd closed her eyes, concentrating, as she gently pressed her pincers against Ar'asha's exoskeleton.

"You know," she said. "Might have felt something like this before." She sat back, but did not take her hand off the Ren'kari. "Ask could I take some medical scans? Could help us understand her condition. Maybe find a way to treat it."

Mon relayed the request, and Ar'asha signed yes. Floyd ran up to the production room, her quick steps echoing, her pale shadow stretching along the floor behind her.

When she returned, she carried a sleek, handheld scanner and a small tube of the nutrient gel. First she scanned the tube. Then she approached Ar'asha with a reverent gentleness, reaching out with the scanner just above the young Ren'kari's exoskeleton.

Ar'asha shied back, almost slipping off the underwater shelf.

"No need to touch," Mon signed. "Okay?"

Ar'asha crept back in place. As Floyd began her scans, Ar'asha started typing again.

"Understand us," she said. "My people are shocked. Humiliated. To us, humans are lesser beings. And now we must beg them for help."

Typical. Understandable. Painful, for them.

Mon wondered how surprised Olve would be at this news. She doublechecked that every typed word of this conversation was being saved.

Floyd finished waving the scanner at the first segment of Ar'asha's exoskeleton and moved on to the next. She didn't seem to notice the arm Ar'asha snuck up to her side, where the gel lay on the floor.

Ar'asha snatched the gel and brought it back toward her chest.

With the fingers of another arm, she flicked the lid up and dipped a single finger into the tube of gel. It smelled like a dusty attic. Ar'asha spread a thin layer of the gel over the area Floyd had just scanned.

The effect was immediate and startling. The gel seemed to melt into her exoskeleton, suffusing the delicate surface with an almost metallic sheen.

Mon leaned closer. It had happened so fast.

Floyd, too, was transfixed by the sight. She scanned the treated area again, her pincers trembling as the data flowed across the screen of her device. She tapped the area very lightly, and then a little harder.

It sounded hard. Like rock.

"The gel repels water," Floyd said. "It will stay there until it wears off or all the nutrient has sunk in."

"How long does the effect last?" Mon asked Ar'asha.

Ren'kari shrugs looked just like human ones.

"Depends," Ar'asha typed. "My shell is weakest. I can never keep up. The ambassador's is strong. Maybe a month."

A month was no time at all.

Floyd lifted the scanner away from Ar'asha, and lifted her gaze to Mon. Floyd's pretty pink eyes were round with wonder. Her wide pink mouth flat with determination.

"Gonna pop these readings on the chat," she said. "See what our medicos think. Maybe we find something better. More permanent than this gel."

Mon nodded, wondering what she could say to get to feel that soft arm, those silky segments, again.

She shook the thought out of her head. Focus.

"In the meantime, we need to make more of this stuff," Mon said and signed, gesturing to the tube of gel. "As fast as we can."

Floyd's expression darkened.

"Gonna be a problem," she said. "Closest bamboo fields were on Apple Island."

Of course they were.

Nothing, apparently, was ever easy on Arkhide.

Mon reached her arm toward Ar'asha. The Ren'kari wrapped an arm around Mon's. Each in her own thoughts.

They sat there that way until it was time for Ar'asha to go.

Chapter Seventeen

The Ren'kari ambassador had not spent even five minutes at the base. Well before the gel was ready and Ar'asha left the cargo cave, the ambassador's discordant notes had faded like a distant argument.

Mon picked up some cold sandwiches and hot tea for three from the kitchen on her way back to the observation lab. The room was still dim, the overhead lights off. The soft glow of the screens casting jagged orange lines across the faces of Aster and Olve.

Already, Floyd had pushed all the data from her medical scans of the Ar'asha to the science chat boards. Along with a two-sentence note: "Green gel temp fix for Ren'kari skeletons. Ideas perm remedy?"

Floyd also told Mon she was trying to goose the synths up top to get more supplies down here fast by threatening to go up the elevator and do it herself. Nobody knew for sure, but it probably wasn't safe for synths to skip the hours-long decompression process. Floyd had smiled at the tizzy that had set the up-top synths into.

But no one was smiling in the lab.

Aster sat in their usual spot at the meeting table, back to the window. Motionless, their face blank with abstraction, they must be diving deep in the WorldNet. Olve slouched in his usual chair, his fingers tapping on the armrest in an agitated rhythm.

"Went that well, did it?" Mon said, setting the tray the tray down with a soft clatter. She grabbed a mug and a sandwich for herself before sinking into her own seat with a huff.

Aster held up a finger, but Olve had the energy to answer.

"The quake at Apple Island damaged part of the Ren'kari city closest to us," he said. "They lost all their stored supplies. We need to double-time gel production."

"And the closest ingredients were on Apple Island," Mon said. She took a bite of the sandwich, some sort of soy-spinach-siracha mash inside flatbread.

Olve's gaze sharpened on her. His face looked thinner than even this morning. Haggard.

"Where have you been?" he said.

Mon finished chewing. She took a sip of tea, sweet and warm and soothing.

"They're not telling you the whole of it."

Aster groaned. Their attention came back to the people in the lab.

"The part we know is bad enough," they said. "A prediction error that shouldn't have happened. Could lead to a potential change in Ren'kari leadership that might change our relationship entirely. And now there's more?"

They made a mug of tea, topped with sugar. They set it in front of Olve with care. Olve accepted the mug without comment, his shoulders sagging as he took a sip.

Mon set the sandwich down. A little dry, even in this humidity.

"Ar'asha came back, to get the last of our gel," she said. She watched the bluster rise behind Olve's eyes. When it was about to spill out down his mouth, she continued.

"The ambassador didn't tell you the half of it."

With a few quick taps, Mon shared the text file of her conversation with Ar'asha, watching as Aster and Olve absorbed the information.

Aster gasped, and looked out to the ocean.

Olve glared at Mon.

"How do you know she's telling the truth?" he said.

"I touched her," Mon said. "But she touched me first! Look at Floyd's report." She flagged the link to that one, since it wasn't in their shared space.

Olve muttered a curse. "Blasted engineer. Sent it out wide."

Mon felt the now-familiar flare of frustration, her fingers tightening around her mug. This time, instead of letting it roll through her and out, she held onto it.

"Well, why the blasted hells not?" she said, her words clipped. "Why don't you ever want to ask for help? You live on a planet with the finest engineering and medical research minds. Sheesh. You actually have people on this planet who are made of the same stuff as the Ren'kari." She gestured to Aster, who nodded in agreement.

"Friendly people," Aster said. "Who like to help. Let them help us."

Olve waved them both away. His hair looked like someone had picked him up, swept the floor with it, and then set him back down.

"Done is done," he said. "Ill-done, but done. But why wouldn't the ambassador have told us, if this was true?"

Mon was too busy rolling her eyes so Aster spoke first.

Aster leaned forward, their expression thoughtful.

"Would you tell 'a lesser race' that your people aren't as strong as they thought? That you actually can't keep them in their place?"

Aster tried to laugh, but it came out a squeak. Mon pointed to the tray, eyebrows raised. Aster poured themselves some tea.

Olve slammed his mug on the table, the sudden noise making Aster flinch.

"They still don't trust us," he said.

"Well, they can't threaten us with annihilation anymore," Aster said. "If they can't come up and get us."

"Not true." Olve returned to tapping on his chair."They could just not tell us when the volcanoes are about to blow. We're so near the population threshold as it is, losing a couple of towns would sink us all."

Mon shivered at the thought. Humans were so fragile. She glanced at Aster, saw the worry creasing their forehead.

"It could be even more complicated than that," Aster said. "We think the Ren'kari have a complex social structure, with different factions and agendas. Maybe the ambassador is trying to protect their own position, or maybe they're afraid of how we'll react if we know the full extent of the crisis."

Mon nodded, closing her eyes to better picture the implications.

"We need to be careful how we handle this," she said. "We don't want to be seen as exploiting their vulnerability."

Olve's head snapped up. Mon startled at the sudden move.

"Why not?" he said. He leaned forward, now tapping on the table. "We can't just sit back and do nothing. We need information. We need to know what we're dealing with."

"I agree," Mon said. "But we need to be smart about it. We've built trust with the Ren'kari. No, we have!" she said as Olve snorted in disbelief. "Patience. Respect. Give them their dignity, even when it's hard."

Aster slid a half a sandwich towards Olve, their movements calm and deliberate. But Olve ignored the offering, his fists slamming down on the table. He glared at Mon.

"Respect?" He said. "They need to respect us. Tell us the truth. As it is, now we'll never know what is going on."

Aster's voice cut through the tension, their tone soothing. "Diplomacy takes time.

"We're out of time," Olve spat out. "Every day we waste trying to play nice is another day the Ren'kari are suffering. We need to get down there. See for ourselves. Then we can help."

Mon blinked, taken aback by the intensity of Olve's words. And their content.

"You want to travel to the Ren'kari city?" Talk about forbidden territory.

Olve's jaw clenched, his fingers curling into fists. "We'd find out the truth," he said. "Get your little friend to invite us. We can't do it without an invitation."

Irritation flared down Mon's limbs. Selfish crank.

"The Ren'kari need supplies," she said. "Not an invasion."

Olve brushed her words aside with a wave of his hand. "A sea rover with two people inside is not an invasion."

Mon looked to Aster, her eyes pleading for help.

"No one is going to the Ren'kari village," Aster said. "We are not asking the young Ren'kari to sacrifice her standing in the society just to ease our curiosity." They held up a top hand, cutting off Olve's next words.

"If—when—we find a cure," Aster continued. "That's when we'll talk to the Ren'kari about letting us in. We need to coexist, Olve. Respect their boundaries."

Olve again opened his mouth to argue, but this time Mon cut him off.

"Aster's right," she said. "We need to find a balance. We need to gather intelligence, yes, but also to build bridges. We need to show the Ren'kari that we're not a threat, that we're partners. Not adversaries."

"Fine," Olve said, still mad. "We'll try it your way. Pretend we're clueless humans only good for making some useless gel that nobody knows what it does. Okay?"

Aster cleared their throat. Their expression grew more grave. The corners of their mouth actually turned down.

"One more thing," they said. "The Cooperative Realm. If they find out about this, if they get involved..."

The thought sent a surge of dread through Mon. She knew the Cooperative, knew their methods. They would stop at nothing to gain control of the situation, to bend the Ren'kari to their will.

And for the synthetic humans like Aster and Floyd, the stakes were even higher. Just existing as a synthetic human was punishable by death in the Cooperative Realm. The genocidal edict was a holdover from the Robot Wars that had nearly torn the galaxy apart. This planet, which traded with the Co-op but did not belong to it, was their last sanctuary. The only place where they could live in peace.

For the Ren'kari, if the Cooperative got involved, it would only be a matter of time before they polluted the oceans, before they pushed aside the boundaries of the carefully negotiated treaties between the Ren'kari and the humans. Before they destroyed everything the Arkhideans had worked so hard to build.

"Stewards of the land," hah.

A bead of sweat trickled down her temple. The dull throb of a headache pounded behind her eyes.

"No," she said. "Nobody's going to let that happen. The Cooperative can never know about this."

Chapter Eighteen

Mon walked out of her room and toward the exercise room, her mind buzzing. Up-top, the finest synthetic and human minds were whirring with theories and tests, trying to figure out the source of the Ren'kari's problem. One chat group was keeping a running list of medical scans for Floyd to perform next time anyone ran into a Ren'kari, which might be tomorrow.

Mon pulled her hair back as she stepped into the room. Despite the room being twice the size of the kitchen area, the air was thick with the tang of sweat and the damp of the cave walls. Too many white lights blazed overhead, casting harsh shadows on the whirring treadmill in the center.

Behind the busy treadmill, one of three, sat a set of weights leaning against a wall of mirrors. In front of the treadmills the wall was painted a serene blue.

Mon glanced at Aster, still lurking in the hall outside the entry to the exercise room. They had pulled her aside as she walked to her room moments earlier, concern etched on their face.

"He's been in there for an hour," Aster had said, their voice low. "I'm worried he's going to hurt himself. Maybe talk to him?"

Mon rolled her shoulders, her mind still processing the news from the Ren'kari. Olve pounded away on the machine in the center of the room, drawing out a sympathetic need in her own muscles. The restlessness that came with being cooped up in this dark cavern under the sea.

Olve huffed in laborious rhythm. His sweat-drenched shirt twisted about his too-thin middle as his skinny legs pumped forward and back. There was a brittleness to his movements, a desperation.

Mon approached the third treadmill, the farthest from the door. As she inspected the machine, she caught a glimpse of Olve's expression—a fleeting look of despair that vanished behind a mask of determination.

Mon's eyes narrowed. She knew that kind of desperation, that need to outrun your own thoughts. She tightened the straps on her running shoes.

Grabbing the handrails, she hoisted herself up and set a steady pace, the machine humming to life beneath her. The familiar burn in her legs was a welcome distraction from the churning in her gut.

And then it wasn't. Mon's heart started hammering, fighting to get air to her pumping legs.

"Slow down," Olve huffed out. "You just got here. Pressure down here is a bitch."

Mon decided to walk the rest of the twenty minutes that she'd set. Maybe knock it down to ten minutes.

A citrus scent fought valiantly against the ever encroaching sweat and grime. Still, it was a room inside a cave. Dank, chill, oppressive if you thought about it. And even if you didn't. Pressure about twenty times that of sea level, no getting away from that.

Which just made Olve's workout that much more of a death

wish. Sure, he was used to it, but really there was no getting used to it.

For a few moments, they ran and walked in silence, the whir of the machines and their synchronized breaths the only out-loud sounds in the room.

"You trying to break that thing?" Mon asked, her tone casual but her eyes sharp.

Olve grunted, not even sparing her a glance.

"What's it to you?"

"Oh, nothing," Mon said, her words clipped between breaths. "Just figured you might want to save some energy for, you know, actually solving this puzzle with the shrimp people."

From the corner of her eye, she saw Olve's jaw clench, a muscle ticking in his cheek. Good. Let him be pissed at her slur on the Ren'kari. Better than watching him self-destruct.

They continued in silence for a few more minutes, the air between them thick with things unsaid. Mon could feel Olve's frustration rolling off him in waves, could see the gears turning in his head even as his body moved on autopilot. She'd seen that same look on the faces of soldiers she'd fought beside, that haunted, hollow-eyed stare that said they were running from something they couldn't escape.

"You know," she said at last, her breath coming in short, hard bursts, "it's not all on you. This mess with the Ren'kari."

Olve pulled the hem of his shirt up and wiped the sweat off his forehead with it. So that's how it got to be so twisted.

"The hell it isn't," he bit out, his voice rough with exertion and emotion. "I'm the expert, right? The one who's supposed to have all the answers?"

Mon snorted, the sound harsh in the close space.

"Yeah, well, newsflash, genius. Nobody has all the answers. Not even the great Olve, master of shrimp linguistics."

The side of her head felt scorched by heat of his glare, but she didn't flinch. She did turn the machine's tension down all the way.

"You think I don't know what it's like?" she pressed, her lungs still burning with the effort. "To feel yourself failing. Everything's falling apart and it's all your fault."

Olve's mouth twisted, his eyes flashing. "You don't know anything about me."

"Maybe not," Mon said. "But I know a thing or two about pressure. About expectations. About the weight of the whole freaking world on your shoulders."

She dragged in a ragged breath, her chest heaving. The words were pouring out of her now, like poison being drawn from a wound. She stopped walking, and the treadmill slowed.

"I've spent my whole adult life following orders, toeing the company line. But you know what? It's all bullshit. Every last bit of it."

Olve's pace faltered, his eyes widening. Mon could see the confusion, the disbelief warring with the anger in his gaze.

"My whole career, I've served Co-op. I'm only now realizing that the Co-op's approach to interspecies relations, to conflict resolution, to most any kind of resolution... it's fatally flawed. Dominance and control, not understanding and cooperation. How dumb was I?"

She jabbed a finger at him, her nail biting into his sweat-slick skin.

"But you know what I do see? I see a chance. A chance to do something different. To be something different. And I'm not going to let you screw it up because you're too busy wallowing in your own bluster and misery."

Olve's mouth opened and closed, his face wide with shock and hurt. Mon felt a twinge of guilt, a flicker of regret.

She pushed it down, buried it deep. She needed him to hear this, to understand.

Olve had slowed to a walk, his breaths evening out. Thank Safra.

"So here's what's going to happen," she said, voice thin but fierce. "You're going to get your shit together. You're going to stop treating the Ren'kari like some kind of science experiment and start seeing them as actual, living, political beings. And you're going to work with me and Aster to figure out a way to fix this mess."

The words hung in the air between them, sharp and searing. Mon felt her heart's pounding in every muscle of her body.

Olve stared at her, his chest heaving, his face a riot of emotions. Anger, confusion, hurt, and something else, something that flickered.

Hope?

"I've been so focused on the language, on the data," he said. "But I've been missing the bigger picture. I…" He swallowed hard, his throat bobbing. "I don't know how to do this. I don't have any of the answers."

Mon felt something inside her soften, just a little. She reached out, her hand hovering over his on the handrail.

"You don't have to do it alone," she said, her voice rough but not unkind. "That's the whole point. We're in this together."

Olve's lips twitched, a ghost of a smile. "Don't have much of a choice, do I?"

Mon snorted, her own lips curving. "Not really, no."

At last, Olve stepped off the treadmill. He grabbed a real towel from the pile in the corner to wipe the sweat from his face.

"Allies, not test subjects," he said. "Partners, not rivals."

Mon grabbed her own towel. Workout definitely over. She reveled in the burn in her muscles, the sweat trickling down her back. It felt good, cleansing. Like shedding an old skin, peeling back the layers of bullshit and pretense to reveal something raw and real beneath.

"We're in this together," she said. "Aster. Floyd. Me. You. Everyone in every blessed chat room, apparently. We'll figure it out."

"We'll figure it out," echoed Olve.

Chapter Nineteen

Next morning, the cargo cave thrummed with activity, everyone doing their part to produce the green gel for the Ren'kari.

The twins, boxy synths with elastic metal arms and upside-down bucket heads, shuttled giant tub after giant tub of the green powder (really white) from the elevators to the processing room. By the time they reached the processing room, they had the exact weight and purity of each box measured and sent to the gel-making machinery.

The three people from ocean research and the one from the trade office scurried around inside the processing room, keeping the two gel-binding machines stocked and counting and packing filled pouches of gel into kegs.

Up-top, collection and processing of the green powder had gone full throttle. The humans of Arkhide had found more bamboo on other islands to replace the grove lost to the tsunami at Apple Island. Overnight, they had built a second processing facility, right on the tiny island above their base.

Every hopper within five hundred kilometers of them was transporting solvents, filters, and workers of all sorts to their island to join the effort. A nearby island was now a campground, filled with yurts and tents and modular kitchens.

Even the newly displaced people from Apple Island were donating some of their own reconstruction supplies to the cause. After all, new bamboo was easy to grow. Ren'kari, apparently, were forever.

In the cave's workshop area, Floyd and Olve paced in tight circles around the screens that drove the industrial-sized printer. All morning they had argued about how to use the materials on hand to make more reasonably good kegs. Next to them were prototypes made of polymers left over from making the last rover, spare furniture, and protein-bar wrappers. One of the wrapper-prototypes, half the normal sized keg, was already being filled as proof of concept. It looked oddly like the shape of Olve's emergency backpack.

Aster roamed the cave floor, mind deep in the WorldNet, keeping track of materials and delivery times. They paced in continuous right-angled triangles, from the doorway of the processing room ("Keep back!") to the pair of elevators ("Out of the way!") to the workshop area ("Stop bugging us!") and down the hypotenuse back to the processing room.

Finally, Aster broke the pattern, stepping out of the long leg of their path to join Mon and Ar'asha at the end of the diving pool. They crouched about a meter away from Mon, who was sitting in front of Ar'asha and chatting as the Ren'kari waited for kegs to be ready.

"Ask her how many of her people are sick," Aster said.

Mon did not roll her eyes.

"Already asked," she said and signed. "All of them, more or less.

Most are okay for now, but at least five thousand are in Ar'asha's position." She pointed to Aster and finger-spelled their name.

Ar'asha repeated the name, and added, "nice to meet you. We call you Four."

Aster's face split into a grin. They stretched all four of their arms and struck a pose.

"Can't imagine why," they said.

Out loud, Ar'asha's laugh sounded like a dolphin chirping. In the range only Mon could hear, it sounded like the popping of metal bubbles.

Mon laughed with her.

"We've been chatting about what the Ren'kari like to do for fun," Mon signed and said aloud. "No surprise, a lot of swimming is involved."

"And music," Ar'asha added.

"Music?" Aster signed.

The Ren'kari's hands moved in a flurry of signs and gestures, so much smoother than just days ago. Ar'asha was a fast learner.

"I can't keep up!" Aster said. "Was that 'grass' or 'boulder'?"

"Boulder," Mon confirmed. "Hollow boulders, metal tubes, and voices. Sing us a song?" she asked Ar'asha.

Ar'asha's luminescence pulsed a rainbow spray of color. Flattered?

She settled herself on the ledge of the pool in a slightly different manner—body more vertical, with more arms to support the position. Slits opened near the edges of her back, almost under the hard shell. Sounds came out.

Ren'kari music—at least the songs that Ar'asha preferred, at least in the air of the cave—were an acquired taste. The honking was bearable, but the sawing-steel parts, especially echoed along the cave walls and ceiling, almost shut down production entirely.

Which was a shame, because the overtones, the parts only Mon could hear, were lovely.

She had to break that code. Get a translation device working so the others could picture it. Mon just bet the math of that music was gorgeous.

"Beautiful," she signed.

"Now you," signed Ar'asha, chiaroscuro eyes winking at Mon.

But not a moment later, her gaze snapped to the far end of the pool. The ocean beyond.

Ar'asha pushed Mon away from the edge of the pool with a force so strong it pushed the Ren'kari deep into the water.

Mon rolled onto her back, but caught herself before going completely over. Reflexes still good, but what in the world? Aster reached for her, to help her up.

Suddenly, the cave shuddered, thundering, sending everyone stumbling. Pouches of gel plopped to the floor, and the lights flickered overhead. The water in the pool roiled. A mini-wave doused both Mon and Aster her. Dank. Sulfuric. Freezing.

The pool went dark. The light through the windows at the cave opening had gone silty brown.

Olve and Floyd rushed over, Floyd grabbing some workshop towels on her way. Mon hoped her sweater and boots were far enough away to have stayed dry.

In case they had to run.

"Checking all the seals," Floyd said.

"Checking up-top," Aster said. "Hope this isn't the start of something bad."

Ar'asha slowly emerged from the pool. She settled even more carefully on the underwater shelf at the end of the pool.

Olve dropped to his knees.

"More shakes coming?" he signed.

"Not now," Ar'asha signed.

"Later?"

"Maybe." Her luminescence gained more reds and purples. Her signs moved closer to her chest, as if she were embarrassed.

Or telling a secret.

"Same fault line as Apple Island, and Mer'kesh," she signed. "Our city. Stronger than expected. Not sure how much stronger." Mon spoke the words for Aster. Floyd draped a towel over Mon's shoulders, a rose-scented embrace.

"Shit," Aster said. "Should we evacuate? Island up-top says they're fine." They looked around. "I don't see any cracks." Mon signed their words for Ar'asha.

"Yet," Olve said and signed.

All four looked at Ar'asha. The adolescent Ren'kari's arms and legs were twining among each other like strands of licorice.

"You should be okay," she signed. But Mon could see the doubt in her words.

And so could Olve. He rolled onto his heels, shooting a panicked glance at Aster.

"What if they're just saying that to ensure the green gel keeps coming?" he said. "I'm beginning to think they consider us expendable."

Ar'asha's patterns flashed yellows.

"You're not!" she signed. "I would warn you."

"Right," Olve said. He pushed to his feet and pulled out his wristcom. "I'm pinging the Ren'kari ambassador, requesting a meeting," he said. "And, since they know all about our forms of communication, also sending a text message along the channel."

"Saying what?" Aster's gaze was distant, distracted. They looked lost. Mon took one of their lower hand in hers. She looked toward Ar'asha.

The Ren'kari must have read her mind. She drew an arm out of the water and wrapped it partway along one of Aster's forearms.

If it wasn't comforting, it was certainly distracting.

"She's warm!" Aster said. "And muscly." They set their top hand on one of Ar'asha's coils. "And wet."

Olve gasped. His face went ashen.

Mon's stomach lurched for the second time in ten minutes.

"So the ambassador does know how to text," Olve said. "Yes, they say. Danger thirty percent and rising. They were waiting to tell us, said they need one more day to confirm. Rift should have stopped days ago, but hasn't yet. At this rate, we start getting bad shakes in two days."

Aster's expression settled into hard focus.

"We can't wait," they said. "We need to send all non-essential personnel up-top now. Decompression takes a day, about. Study team should start now, to make it through the stages."

Olve shook his head.

"No, we all go up. We can make the gel on the surface." He turned to Ar'asha. "Can you get to the elevator and retrieve the kegs?" he signed.

Ar'asha's limbs flickered with apology, her sign heavy with regret. "No."

Floyd gripped Mon's shoulders from behind. She was wearing her human-style hands today.

"Me and the twins can stay," Floyd said. "We're true synths, no soft bits. Could survive a cave-in."

"Bullshit," Aster said. "You're plenty soft. And no, none of you is expendable."

Mon reached for the strap of her emergency backpack, now hidden under Floyd's towel. Still there.

"I don't want to leave," Mon said. "Especially if we might have to come right back down. Isn't this exactly what these packs are for?"

Aster grimaced. "They're for air emergencies, not cave-ins."

As the debate raged on among the humans, Ar'asha watched intently. But as Mon got more and more drawn in, and the conversation turned into rapid fire, she stopped signing to the Ren'kari.

Ar'asha tapped Mon's knee.

"Wait," Mon said to the others.

"There's another cave, farther from here," Ar'asha signed. "Safer. I could take someone to see it."

"Why don't we know about it, then?" Olve said and signed. He crouched to Ar'asha's level again.

"Too close to Ren'kari," Ar'asha said. "This one here is good for you and us both."

"But the other one is good for us, too?" Olve said. He looked expectantly at Aster.

Who recoiled.

"Absolutely not," they said. "Two days is not enough to move a base."

"Dunno," Floyd said. "Might be." She counted something out on the fingers of one pink-nail-polished hand. "Not that many trips. For the basics."

"Not and keep making the green gel," Aster said, glaring at her. "Besides, we need to know exactly where she's taking us. Make her give us the exact coordinates."

Ar'asha looked at Mon, not understanding.

"Show us on the map?" Mon signed, pointing at the paired tablet.

Olve changed the tablets to map display. Ar'asha pointed to a spot roughly twenty kilometers away.

Olve frowned. "Looks ideal. See, there's even tunnels between the caves. Easy to seal. There's gotta be something wrong with it."

Aster pointed to a spot on the map a short distance away.

"Because their other city is right there, remember?" they said. "It would have put us too close. Uncomfortably close."

Mon looked to Aster, an idea forming.

"Can we get someone up-top to check it out?"

As Aster started messaging his transportation colleagues up-top, Olve shook his head.

"They won't be able to tell from the surface," he said. "I'll go."

"No!" Aster's voice was sharp with fear and frustration. "At least ask the ambassador first."

Ar'asha, her understanding of human nonverbal communication growing by the minute, quickly signed to Mon. "Tell them only you can go."

Mon hesitated. She'd been dying to take one of those rovers out for a spin. Couldn't be that much different than hoppers or short-hop planes, right?

But what did she know of siting bases?

"I'll go," she signed, and said out loud. "But someone else has to come, too. Someone who knows the base inside and out."

All eyes turned to Floyd, who blinked in surprise. "What?"

Chapter Twenty

Mon stepped into the sea rover and smelled cherries. Floyd must have piloted it last.

With only four bucket seats and an equal amount of open space in the back, the rover was smaller than the same-style hoppers for air travel. With its transparent domed roof and the two wide rudders on each side of its wide round body, it earned its "turtle" nickname.

The sleek lines and friendly surfaces inside showed the playful ingenuity of Arkhide's engineers. As Mon settled into the co-pilot's seat, she couldn't help but run her fingers over the floating control screens. Such clear displays—icons, understandable even to non-Arkhidean speakers. Such a soft, responsive touch.

But on the floor between the pilots' seats sat two old-fashioned joysticks, just in case.

Floyd sealed the hatch behind them, the soft hiccup of the double airlock a reminder that they weren't going up in the air, but into water.

Water under immense pressure.

Couldn't be that different than vacuum, right?

Right.

The rover whirred to life, batteries engaging with a crackle and then a steady hum. The oxygen recyclers whistled reassuringly. Floyd pulled the two screens to float right in front of her and ran her hands along the controls, following a familiar pattern of pre-flight checks everywhere.

Mild panic flashed through Mon's shoulders and fingers. She was usually the one piloting. To just sit here felt wrong. She should be the one doing the checks.

But what did she know of sea currents? Before now, she'd never been deeper than maybe ten meters under the sea.

Mon swallowed, her mouth dry. Thinking like that could terrify a person.

Floyd's serene confidence was a balm. The synth's hot-pink-tipped fingers owned the screens. Her sharp eyes checked every seal, window, and door.

Mon sighed, and fixed her safety straps. She left a little give so she could lean out in case anything fun showed up.

As they sank into the pool, the lights dimmed as if they were sinking into some of that thick green gel. Mon couldn't see anything.

A flicker of primal fear—this small, squishy self trapped in this tiny metal shell, pressed in by tons of water on all sides.

But then, colors, and movement, caught her eye, and fear turned to wonder. Ar'asha swam alongside the rover, her happy bioluminescent chatting casting colorful patterns through the murky water.

The Ren'kari's movements were graceful on land, but in the water they were poetry. Her long back tentacles—legs—kicked hard from time to time and then trailed behind her like the train of a gown. Her shorter, thinner upper tentacles—arms—reached here and there, as if collecting information like cherries and placing them into an imaginary basket near her belly.

Mon couldn't speak, her throat tight with every emotion. Ar'asha could be alien, and yet so familiar. So beautiful. Her movements a dance, light and motion and deep meaning.

Floyd had a route programmed in, but Ar'asha re-routed them almost immediately.

"This way," she signed, her other arms fanning and shimmying to her sides. She floated a bit up and then rocketed away.

"Ha!" Floyd's laugh was infectious. "Good guide. Knows the currents."

Whenever Mon had seen the ocean through the windows of the lab, the underwater world looked like an odd sort of oil painting. In the rover, though—inside the water—it was like being inside a shaken-up snow globe.

Schools of shiny fish darted one way and then another in dizzying patterns. Arm-long eels tried to follow the pattern, probably hoping for a snack. Good luck.

Plankton and loose plant life drifted down like soft rain, most browns and greens but some luminescent. Caught in the rover's floodlights, they sparkled. Jellylike organisms drifted by or, caught in the current, surfed like comets, their delicate tendrils trailing like ghostly streamers.

To their right rose the mountain that housed their cave base. Up-top it was just a tiny island, but down here it joined with others to form a range that traveled as far as Mon could see. Gray rock with veins of dark reds and dull silvers.

"Incredible," Mon said.

Floyd chuckled. "Just wait." Her smile grew even wider.

"You're glad to get out here, aren't you?" Mon said.

Floyd shot her a guilty look. "Not my job, anymore."

Mon scoffed. "Down here, it's everyone's job."

"Tell Aster that," Floyd said. She was one of the warm synths. Between Floyd and Mon, the small cabin was growing quite cozy.

Ar'asha stayed a bit in front of them. She would pause at spots —a valley in the mountains, a rather large stack of coral—where they might veer off the wrong way. When the rover made the right choice, Ar'asha shot ahead again.

The Ren'kari's agile form was perfect for barreling ahead at speed. Her limbs trailed behind her like the fins of a shark. She cut through the water like a laser, her bioluminescence keeping up a steady chatter.

"Thermal vent ahead," Ar'asha signed, her patterns flashing excitement. "Water is warmer. Attracts many creatures."

Mon relayed the information to Floyd.

"Check it out on the way back," Floyd said. "Don't tell Aster." She winked.

Mon could barely feel the rover straining against the force of the water. Just the slightest creaks and groans as the metals and other composites adjusted to their speed and the ever-present pressure.

At another pause, Ar'asha pointed out to their left. "Other Ren'kari city that way. Smaller."

Mon couldn't see anything. Which, of course, was because it was at least two hundred more meters down.

Someday, maybe, the Ren'kari would invite humans for a visit. Maybe Olve.

Maybe Heather.

As they neared the coordinates of the new cave, the seascape around them began to open up, the rocky outcroppings and deep crevices worn smoother than at the base. This part of the ranges must be much older. Deep crevices snaked through the rock, their depths lost in shadow, hinting at the vast, unexplored spaces that lay beyond.

Ar'asha swam ahead of the rover, her light patterns flowing with blues and oranges as she directed them towards a dark opening shaped like a half-yawn.

Edges crumbling, the space looked like a careless giant had scooped it out for a shelf. Or maybe the net for a monster game of water polo.

The rover's floodlights clawed into the thick, inky dark beyond the cave's mouth. Mon couldn't tell if the shiver that shook her spine was excitement or fear.

"Depth one eighty," Floyd said.

"Twenty meters difference?" Mon said.

"Twenty-one-five," Floyd nodded. She'd pulled up another screen, with survey data "Equipment would work fine. Running the checklist. Aster, copy?"

"I hear you, Floyd," Aster said into Mon's ear, and probably straight to Floyd's brain. "We're all listening and watching, but just I will talk."

The rover was equipped with the usual suite of sonar, visual, and acoustic sensors—and a baby drone. Floyd released it and sent it into the cave, close to one of the walls. In almost no time, they had enough data to form a holographic display.

The outline of an intricate web of tunnels and caves stretched out before them.

"Bit of a maze," Mon said.

"Olve's right," Aster said from the base. "Good for air seals. We wanted that. Wonder why they didn't offer it as an option."

"Too close to Ren'kari town," Floyd said. "NIMBYs."

Mon ran her own checks, her eyes scanning the readouts with a practiced eye. The rover's hull was intact, the pressure seals holding strong against the crushing weight of the water outside. The cameras and other sensors primed and ready to capture every detail of the space.

Outside the rover, Ar'asha swam in eager circles, her signs conveying a sense of urgency and anticipation.

"I found it!" she signed.

Strange that her people's emissaries had not.

"Ready to go, base," Floyd said. Request confirmation."

There was a moment of silence, a pause that stretched out like an eternity. Then Aster's voice, calm.

"Confirmed," they said.

As they crossed the threshold of the cave, the rover's floodlights flickered and dimmed, the external cameras struggling with the inky black.

The darkness embraced them.

Chapter Twenty-One

Floyd guided the rover into the cave, slow and careful. The turtle vessel's floodlights pushed the inky dark away only for a few meters.

Goosebumps rose along Mon's arms. She rubbed at them irritably.

It was plenty warm here in the rover. And the holographic map their drone had provided showed that there was nothing big and moving. Nothing. And she had gone into scarier caves—lots scarier—looking for traces of lost civilizations with her astroarcheologist parents.

But those had been above the water. She wouldn't be able to use her feet to flee anything that came to bite her here.

The cave was made of the same gray rock, shot through with thin veins of minerals, as their base. Its floor had some serious peaks, but nothing a little smart architecture couldn't deal with.

The opening wasn't representative of the cave, though. Its short shelf soon opened into a much bigger space. Cathedral high, but skinny.

The drone, way above them and to the right, illuminated a vast world of tiny life along that wall. Twisted forms like ghost coral pulsed and writhed with itty bitty fish, dancing plants, and shrimpy things that could be Ar'asha's baby cousins.

"Get closer?" Mon breathed, as if speaking too loud would startle the miniature world. She wanted to see what made the leaves on the plants move.

Floyd tip-toed the rover a little closer.

"Natural aquifers," she said. "Filtration systems would be a breeze."

Ar'asha was already halfway through this cave, her voice blues and oranges. Then a yellow.

She scooted back to the rover.

"Geothermal vents!" she signed, the pattern of her biolumines-cence adding another exclamation point. "Two. See." She scooted back to where she'd been.

Floyd floated the rover toward the Ren'kari, slow and careful. The two vents, only as wide as Mon's hand, were what was causing the current. And drawing the whole tiny, colorful world of crea-tures into this cave.

"Biologists would piss themselves," Floyd said. "To get to watch this out their window all day."

Mon frowned in surprise. "Not use them for energy?"

"Nah," Floyd backed the rover up, getting out of the current and out of the way of the plankton and crawly shrimp. "Got lots of choices for power. Never another chance to learn about this."

Ar'asha was ahead of them again, her arms a rainbow of flick-ering lights. Curious, contented. She'd found one of the narrow passages.

She darted in, and quickly back out. "Too small for you, but bigger later," she signed. They'd already decided that this was a drone reconnaissance. Any readings they got were gravy. Floyd wasn't taking any chances with her rover.

They swept in a wide semicircle, finding the three passages the drone had mapped. Everything looked good to Mon. But what did she know?

"What do you think?" she asked Floyd.

Aster answered, in her ear. "Looking really good. Get us pictures over to the left, where the dip in the floor is."

As they neared the dip, really just an indentation about a half-meter lower than the main part of the floor, Mon's breath caught. There, nestled in a bed of soft, gray sand, wriggled a cluster of small, white creatures.

Long and slender, their bodies nearly translucent blue, they had a mass of writhing tentacles at one end. At the other end, a tiny mouth with a perfect circle of icicle-shaped teeth.

"Baby eels?" Floyd asked. She tipped the rover forward, aiming the lights into the space.

"We're checking our database," Aster said. "Weird that they're not by the vents. They look so fragile."

"Kinda cute." Floyd smiled as one eel grabbed another by the middle; the "prey" kicked its attacker off with a whip-flick of its body.

Mon snorted. "Yeah, just stay away from the bitey ends." She found herself leaning forward, as if that would get her closer to the little creatures.

"Olve just heard from the ambassador," Aster said. "They say the cave is inappropriate and we should leave immediately."

Spoilsports.

Mon tapped the rover's clear dome to catch Ar'asha's attention. The Ren'kari floated just above the nest, to all appearances as entranced as Floyd.

"Are they making sounds?" she signed to the Ren'kari. Ar'asha drifted closer, her patterns flickering with a whispering light. She reached out with one arm, sharp fingertips hidden. She stroked the wriggling things with a delicate, almost reverent touch. They seemed to respond to her presence, their wriggling intensifying, their toothy maws opening and closing as if they were singing.

"No sound," Ar'asha signed with two other of her arms. "So cute!"

"We'll have to find a new home for them," Mon said. "If we do decide to set up a base here, we can't just uproot them."

"Stick 'em by the vents," Floyd said. "Let 'em make friends."

Floyd eased back from the nest and started to turn the rover toward the entrance. Mon reached for her hand, to ask her to wait just another minute, but Aster's voice startled her into silence.

"Get out of there," they said, voice rising.

"Hear you," Floyd said, completing the turn. "Checking out the side wall on our way."

"Now," Aster said. "Something big is coming your way."

Floyd frowned. "Shouldn't we wait, then?"

Mon looked for Ar'asha. The Ren'kari was reluctantly following. Her colors pulsed calm.

And then shifted to fast, brilliant, staccato.

Ar'asha shot away from the nest, past the rover, toward the mouth of the cave. As she passed, her arms frenzied, she signed, "Go! Go!"

Floyd punched the speed up, but not much. A smart pilot, she wouldn't push speed in a new environment. She skimmed the floor, staying close to the wall. Aiming straight at the dim gray oval of the cave's outer shelf.

"Belts tight," she said, her fingers twitching, making micro changes in the rudders to keep them aligned. Must not be using the backup autopilot.

They had just reached the opening when a massive shadow

loomed out of the depths. Long, thick, swallowing the very light around it.

It was shaped like a baby eel, but gargantuan. Its body a mass of muscle and sinew, its maw a gaping, needle-toothed abyss. Mom couldn't see where its eyes were, but it was coming straight at them.

"Uh-oh," Floyd said. "Mom."

Then it started to turn. The ocean's faint light returned as the long, long body passed. It must need to bank to slow, so it didn't crash into the cave entrance. It was so wide Mon didn't see how it even fit through.

She didn't want to be here when it tried.

Without thinking, Mon reached for the controls that weren't there. Pilot instincts no good when you're not the pilot. She gripped the armrests on her chair instead. Her fingers still twitched, as if correcting their course.

Floyd pushed the rover full forward. As soon as it picked up speed, she turned the lights off and powered everything down.

"Can't outrun it," she said. "Gonna play dead."

Smart. And terrifying.

With all the familiar noises gone, the world went eerily silent. The mama eel did not have a resonance. Mon felt the blindness of her Listener senses like a wound to her mind.

The rover's momentum took it past the shelf, already drifting down and away.

But not soon enough.

In the midst of its graceful arc, the mama eel stiffened. It whipped its long body into an exclamation point aimed straight at them.

Sweet Safra's ghost. The thing was all teeth.

Mon tasted blood. Must have bitten her cheek.

Ar'asha drifted from above to put herself between the eel and the rover. She, too, wasn't moving. Even her colors were off. Mon didn't know they could do that.

Playing dead.

But putting herself in danger.

The mama eel swung its massive head from side to side as it tried to locate the rover. Its maw gaped open, revealing another row of jagged, knife-like teeth behind the first thick row.

But the thing couldn't seem to find them.

Please.

Mon's breathing was so shallow she felt dizzy. The air circulator was off, but they had plenty for now. But she wasn't about to make any new noise, even the slightest whiff of an inhale.

Please.

Floyd used the joystick to tap the rudder, to keep the rover turned to face the threat. No power necessary. Her other hand hovered in front of Mon, like a parent trying to protect a child just before a crash.

Mon wished that made her feel more comforted.

Then the monster eased up.

It returned to its slow circle toward the cave.

In the silence, Mon heard Floyd swallow. She did the same. They both inhaled, shallow.

Heading into the cave, the eel's jagged maw passed within two meters of them.

Within one meter of Ar'asha.

Its passing, even slowed, it buffeted the rover so much Floyd had to grab the joystick with both hands to keep them from spinning like a top. Ar'asha spun a little, but kept her place between them and the mama eel.

As its head entered the cave, Mon groaned in relief.

It slid like in the entrance had been specially built for it. No clearance.

When it was halfway in, Mon released her grip on the armrests. Too soon.

As the last of its length entered the cave, the mama eel gave a little flick of its tail segment. A push to shove itself all the way in.

The tail took the rover on the side, full force, like a bat hitting a ball over the fence.

The rover slammed into the mountain.

Mon's head snapped, but her seat restraints held. There'd be bruising there. Her vision was all red stars.

The only sound was the creaking of the hull and the thundering of Mon's heartbeat. She reached out blindly, her hand finding Floyd's warm knee.

Floyd already her hands back on the control screens, powering everything up. The warm, familiar buzzes and overtones returned.

"Floyd!" roared Aster's voice through the comm.

"Okay," Floyd said through gritted teeth. "Okay. One rudder down. No leaks. Okay."

Thank Safra for that.

Mon blinked the stars out of her vision. Everything still seemed blurry. The water outside was a fog of plankton and gray sand, stirred up by the mama eel's passing.

A nice hot cocoa would be fine right now.

And to get out of this rover.

"You're okay, really?" she whispered to Floyd.

Floyd spared a moment to rest her hand on Mon's.

"We're both okay," she said. "Scanners say so. Let's go home."

Ar'asha.

Mon stood without thinking, trying to see as far as possible. The seat straps slammed her down.

"Ar'asha!" she said.

Floyd froze for a fraction of a second. Then her hands raced along the scanner control panels. Searching, searching.

Mon saw her first. Just above them, closer to the rock, dangling in the misty water. Her body hadn't rebounded from the mama eel's slap as far as the rover had.

What was left of her body.

Ar'asha's exoskeleton had shattered under the force of the impact. Along its cracks, the bioluminescence flickered oddly, as if it had lost the mind controlling it.

Her arms and legs floated without intention. Their colors random, and fading.

Her chiaroscuro eyes, dimming.

Chapter Twenty-Two

Mon held her breath watching Floyd maneuver the sea rover's net around Ar'asha's limp body. When one of the two mechanical arms holding the net gently pushed the Ren'kari, to float her farther from the edges of the rock that had cracked her shell, Mon winced.

The Ren'kari floated without intention. Colors were still flashing along Ar'asha's dangling limbs, but in not in any clear pattern. Different patterns on different limbs. That couldn't be good.

The rover's net, another Arkhidean marvel, was designed to collect delicate undersea samples. Its gossamer-thin filaments strong enough to lift a small submersible. But as the net wrapped itself around Ar'asha's battered body, it looked woefully inadequate. Such a flimsy barrier against the vast, mocking sea.

The Ren'kari's bioluminescence remained in the purple-blue range, pulsing slowly. Not dead, but certainly not well.

With a deft flick of her wrist, Floyd guided the net towards the rover's airlock. The pincers at the end of the rover's mechanical arms were bigger versions of the pincher hands Floyd had on yesterday. Small wonder she was expert.

As Floyd started pulling in the net, Mon unclipped her restraints and clomped to the back of the rover. Her legs seemed to have gone to sleep. Stupid water pressure. By the time she reached the airlock, the outer hatch had already opened, the internal space between the hatches filling with water.

Heart in her throat, Mon gripped the handholds by the inner door. The girl had tried to save them. They couldn't let her die.

Through the door's small window, she could see the white of the net, and the shadow of Ar'asha. The pincers swept the net inside. They latched it somehow top and bottom. Giving the Ren'kari more cushion during movement.

The outer door sealed shut with a dull clang that reverberated through the rover's hull. The flat, lifeless sound made an eerie counterpoint to the lively chirps and trills of the young Ren'kari.

"Got her," Floyd said on the open communications channel. "Twenty-five minutes out."

Mon touched her mic on. "Can we take her to that city nearby? Aster?"

"Olve asked," Aster said. "We're waiting on the message now."

"City's twenty minutes closer," Floyd said. "Better."

Mon pressed her palm against the viewport, the reinforced glass cold and unyielding beneath her touch. Beyond, shadows played across Ar'asha's still form. The sight of the young Ren'kari suspended in the water, still and silent, chilled Mon's blood.

She flicked on the overhead light in the airlock. Ar'asha would want to see where she was. The sight made Mon gasp, as if one of the mama eel's teeth had lanced through her chest.

The girl's carapace was a bit battered, but along her back many of the segments had cracked. Some were missing chunks. Mon could see sinew underneath. Soft parts that should never be exposed to the elements.

How could they put that back together again?

The Ren'kari would know. This must be a common event, back-cracking, right?

A click on the comms, and Aster's voice came on.

"Ambassador says no." Aster's normal musical tone was harsh. "Says bring the body back to the base and they'll pick it up tomorrow."

The body?

"Tell them she's still alive," Mon said.

"We did," Aster said.

"Tell them again!"

Floyd popped a panel open and pulled out a scanner. She handed it back to Mon. Mon fumbled with it until she figured it out. Super sleek medical scanner.

Mon pressed the device against the viewport and set it to wide scan. The pitch of its electronic whirrs and waves set her teeth on edge.

The readout flickered and danced, a maddening array of numbers and symbols that meant nothing and everything.

"Sending medical data now," Floyd said.

"Receiving," Aster said.

Mon pushed back her wayward hair. Her scalp was too hot. She could smell the gel she used to tame it, honeysuckle summer, but the stupid stuff wasn't doing anything.

Ar'asha was in critical condition.

They had no idea how to help her. They had ideas, sure, but no proof anything would work.

She—and Floyd—were the only people any Ren'kari had ever even touched. And she had no idea. Maybe Floyd did.

Aster's response was swift. "Critical condition, best we can tell."

"We have to take her to her people," Mon said, fear a fishhook tugging at her heart. "They'll know how to help her. They have to."

"Hang on, Ar'asha," she murmured to the airlock door. To her strange, luminous friend.

Floyd got the rover out of the silt and back on the path they'd taken to get here. Mon's mind raced with possibilities, each more desperate than the last. They could drop the 200 meters in half a minute, hand Ar'asha to waiting medics, and then slowly rise to avoid the chance of decompression sickness.

They could drive straight down into the city and drop Ar'asha off at the biggest dwelling they saw. Force the Ren'kari to care for her.

They could get the Ren'kari to send medical instructions to the humans. At least enough to stabilize Ar'asha. The Ren'kari wouldn't be too pig-headedly private to share that information, could they?

"Floyd," Aster was back. "Come straight to base. All speed."

"What did they say?" Mon said. "Are they meeting us there?"

Aster's hesitation was answer enough.

"No, Mon. They're not."

The words punched Mon in the gut, driving the air from her lungs. She slid to the floor of the rover.

She couldn't get the words out.

Floyd picked them up. "What do you mean, they're not?" she said. "They can't just abandon her!"

"The ambassador says... they say Ar'asha's injuries are fatal."

Mon's vision swam. Hot tears chilled as soon as they touched her cheeks.

"No," she ground out through the spasming of her throat. "Her lights are on. She might be disabled, but she doesn't have to die."

"Mon." Aster used the talking-to-a-child tone everyone hated. "Disabled may mean death, down here. We don't know their culture. We have to respect that."

No they didn't.

Mon felt the rover lurch, heading home at speed. Floyd's hand found her shoulder, their grip strong and steady.

"Mon," they said softly. "Buckle up."

On the comms line, Aster cleared their throat.

"It's bad, with the Ren'kari. The ambassador said Ar'asha is the fourth casualty. Usually they have a death every decade or so. The Ren'kari, they're overwhelmed, Mon. They're trying to shore up their city to keep the living Ren'kari safe."

"She's alive!" Mon's shout scraped her lungs. "I hear her. We can't just... we can't just give up on her."

The silence that followed was heavy, broken only by the hum of the rover's engines, the overtones of the life-support systems, and the slightest of hums from Ar'asha on the Listener spectrum.

What could they do? What hope did they have, against the vast indifference of the ocean? Against the cold calculus of her people?

"We are not letting her die," Mon said, her voice low and fierce. "We're going back to base. And we're going to find a way to save her."

Floyd's grip on her shoulder tightened, a silent affirmation.

"Aster, we need you to get everything ready. Medical supplies, equipment, whatever you can find. We need your help."

"On it," Aster said. "But hurry. And keep taking the med readings. So we know what to expect."

As the rover surged forward, the water churning in its wake,

Mon closed her eyes, reaching out with every fiber of her being, every Listener cell in her body.

Reaching for Ar'asha, for the fragile thread of connection that had brought them together.

Chapter Twenty-Three

By the time the sea rover reached the cargo cave, Mon was both exhausted and buzzing with panic.

Ar'asha's medical readings hadn't changed, which could be good or bad. Nothing was oozing from her back, where the jagged bits of broken shell seemed to pulse. But her big oval eyes weren't whirring, weren't focusing. And she wasn't communicating.

The Ren'kari didn't seem aware of her surroundings, which could be bad or good. Waking up trapped inside an airlock in a human sea rover would be a mighty shock.

Mon dug her fingernails into the bottom seal of the small, chilly window in the airlock's inner door. She should go sit in one of the seats, but Floyd's piloting was ghostly smooth.

And she didn't want to leave Ar'asha.

She longed to touch Ar'asha. To comfort her. Was she cold? Was she shaking? But of course the airlock was filled with water, which must be good for her, right? Even if it was impossible for humans.

Mon couldn't seem to breathe right anymore. Her breaths hitched and hiccuped. Or she forgot to breathe altogether. Usually she was good in emergencies, calm and creative. But this—

"Slow way down," Aster said over the comms. "We've put a room for her in the pool, at the near corner. Don't hit it! But try to get the rover's airlock as near it as possible."

Floyd flipped the three working rudders around, using their drag to stem the rover's speed. Mon had to grab the handholds beside the airlock door to stay upright.

Floyd slid the rover close to the far edge of the pool's entrance, the bottom half of the flat circle of the cave's mouth. She coasted, slow, into the moon pool and then nosed the rover up. Coming out of the water was the reverse of going in. From murk and thick noise to clear air and familiar harmonies.

As soon as the rover's dome broke the water line, Mon saw the makeshift medical area. A clear cube a shade taller than Aster on each side was suspended half in the pool's water, half out. Two sides were mostly giant sealable doors, one facing the edge of the pool, the other opposite it, facing them.

An airlock, just like the one that led in and out of the lab upstairs.

Clever. Inside, Ar'asha would be able to stay safely moist while still giving the humans access to her wounds.

On the pool's deck, two of the long tables from the workshop had been scooted to within arm's reach of the clear box. Mon saw the usual medical supplies, but also a printer-fabricator, and a pile of what looked like metal or plastic sticks. Next to the tables were two kegs for the green gel, their tops off.

Inside the box, at the outer open door, Aster stood in water up to their waist. Waiting for Ar'asha.

Olve, on the other side of the supply tables, had two massive floating screens up. One was chock full of text, scrolling fast. The other showed the outline of a Ren'kari, with red marks all along their back.

The twins were hauling yet more supplies and arranging them on the tables.

They were ready to help. All of them.

Mon's chest eased. Tears pushed out of her eyes. She took a deep breath.

They would do all they could.

All of them.

Floyd rotated the rover, aligning the airlock with the open door to the emergency-room box. Aster shook their head but didn't say anything. They must be talking on their private link. Floyd stopped a half meter from the doorway.

"Ready," Floyd said to Mon. "Open the outer door."

Mon tapped the controls, and the door slid open. Water rushed out of the top of the space, exposing Ar'asha up to the base of her carapace. Ar'asha, cocooned in the rover's net, did not move.

Aster, wearing surgical gloves and carrying a diving knife, reached up and cut the cord where the net had been tied at the top of the airlock. The net spread open so easily that they could push it down and away from Ar'asha without snagging her.

They stowed the knife, and reached for something behind them that looked like a short sawhorse, two upside-down Vees for legs with a flat, narrow crossbeam connecting them. The crossbeam sat just underneath the waterline. Aster pushed the contraption partway out of the door, leaving one set of legs resting on the floor of the box.

They leaned forward, reaching through Ar'asha's dangling arms, trying not to disturb them. The colors on the Ren'kari's arms did not change, still inky blue and rust red and bruise purple.

Aster's hands reached the side edges where Ar'asha's exoskeleton met the meat of her. They lifted her the way a mother would a human baby from a highchair, fingers wide under the arms.

Mon longed to get to the other side of the airlock. Help them. She wiped at her face.

So, so carefully, Aster pulled Ar'asha forward. Over the weird sawhorse, and then onto it, belly along the flat top. The width was perfect for her, leaving all her limbs free.

As Aster pulled the sawhorse all the way into the box, Ar'asha's dozen arms and legs trailed behind. Some made it into the box on their own. Aster gently corralled the rest, sweeping them into the enclosure. They were saying something to the Ren'kari. Probably something soothing.

As soon as Ar'asha was settled, Aster pulled the door shut. They scooted around Ar'asha and out the other side.

It took only a couple of minutes for Floyd to maneuver the rover into its dock and Mon to purge the water out of the airlock. But the time seemed to stretch forever.

Finally she was out, and running toward the makeshift emergency room. The air carried the tang of saltwater and the sharp, chemical scent of antiseptic, a jarring contrast that made her nose itch and her eyes water.

But as she drew closer, she slowed. Ar'asha's shattered exoskeleton looked even worse in the clear blue-white lights the twins had just turned on. A jagged ruin of splintered siliconate chitin. Half-exposed to the air on the makeshift table, the wounds were, indeed, oozing some thick substance. Ar'asha's limbs hung lifeless in the water like fronds of seaweed.

But at least they were moving, a little. Something inside Ar'asha still pulsed.

Aster had joined Olve in front of the giant screens.

"Tell me what to do," Mon said as soon as she reached them, the words sandpaper as they passed her throat.

Olve glanced at her, and then quickly back to the screens. His fingers danced, his gaze skimming a series of readouts, his brow furrowed.

Aster was more forthcoming.

"Her shell did what it was supposed to. It took the blow, and softened the impact on her inner sections. Saved her life. But what we can't figure out is why it broke."

They pointed at the screen showing the outline of Ar'asha. When Aster touched the shell, a window opened up showing its composition and other data.

"Look," they said. "Based on simple composition, it should have been able to withstand far more pressure. She lives at four hundred meters below, for bloody instance."

"That's an effect of the sickness, then?" Mon said. "That and the gray color?"

"Hundred to one odds." Aster looked over to Ar'asha, sighing. "And probably why they didn't want us to try to save her. Now we know."

Olve swiped a window away with his hand and a growl.

"Later," he said. "Now look: The damage seems to be primarily to her exoskeleton into the first layer of underlying muscle. We need to check for signs of internal bleeding or organ damage."

Mon swallowed hard. "Okay. How?"

Olve hesitated, his gaze eyes flicking to the scrolling chat screen. "Consensus best guess is first to try to stimulate the nerve clusters at the base of the tentacles. Lack of response signals something's wrong down the line."

"But isn't that where Aster was holding her?"

"Not just touch. It has to be a pinch. Something sudden."

"I'll do it." Leaning into the box trying to avoid the water, Mon tasted the iron mix of hope and dread. She gazed at the still, silent form of the young Ren'kari. The thought of causing her any more pain, any more suffering, was almost too much to bear.

But she had to help her. To help, they had to know what was wrong.

With trembling fingers, Mon reached out, her hand hovering near the soft, fleshy underside of Ar'asha's nearest arms. She took a deep breath, steeling herself for what was to come.

Mon brushed her fingers against the solid, lukewarm skin. She took in a breath and held it. Apologized in advance to Ar'asha.

Pinched the underside, hard.

Nothing. No response, no flicker of movement.

Mon moved to another limb.

Again, nothing.

But then, just as she was about to pull away, she felt it. A tiny, almost imperceptible twitch, a flutter of movement so faint that she might have missed it if she hadn't been looking for it.

She hadn't done it hard enough, the first time.

"Positive response," Mon breathed, her voice trembling. "And the colors changed, briefly."

Floyd stepped up behind Mon. She held a different scanner in her hands. With it, she scanned Ar'asha front to back, top to bottom.

Mon watched, transfixed, as a three-dimensional hologram of Ar'asha's body flickered to life in over by Aster and Olve. A ghost-like image that rotated as if alive.

Mon rested her hand on Ar'asha's arm.

"Be right back."

When Floyd's scans were complete, they could see the damage at any angle. The underside of Ar'asha's exoskeleton was a spiderweb of cracks and fissures that ran the length of her body.

But it was the sight of her internal structures that made Mon's breath catch. Beneath the shattered shell, Ar'asha's muscles and organs pulsed with a soft, steady glow, a bioluminescent tapestry of light and color that was unlike anything she had ever seen.

"Look at that," Aster breathed.

"Like a galaxy in there," Floyd said.

Mon could only nod, her throat tight. She reached out with trembling fingers, tracing the lines of Ar'asha's body in the hologram. Parts of the Ren'kari's physiology were a mystery, others looked kind of similar to ones she'd learned in school.

"First thing," Aster said. "We coat her wounds with the nutrient gel. If I'm right," they waved at the window of scrolling text, "and consensus says I might be, the gel could stabilize her. Give us more time to help."

"Couldn't hurt, probably," Olve said. Mon glanced at him, and then took a longer look. Hair tangled, one eye twitching, skin clammy. Not good.

Aster pulled an armful of the gel dispenser packets out of a keg. They shoved half in the pockets of their coveralls and handed the rest to Mon.

"Help?"

Mon took the packets and turned back to Ar'asha, her too still, too silent friend. Aster stepped into the water and started at the back. Mon took the front.

With a touch as soft as a whisper, she spread the gel on the shattered remnants of the Ren'kari's exoskeleton. Her fingers smoothed the oddly shimmering substance over the jagged edges and gaping fissures.

Aster was right. No way a shell this thick should have shattered. At its shallowest, the exoskeleton was two of Mon's fingers wide. Should have gotten dented, at most.

The scent of the gel filled the air in the little compartment. A heady mix of brine and something sweet and floral, like the nectar of a newly discovered flower. It clung to Mon's skin, felt a little buzzy. Water bubbled on top of it but didn't soak in.

As she worked, Mon could feel the warmth of Ar'asha's body beneath her fingers. Could see the faint, flickering pulse of her bioluminescence. Could sense her faint familiar overtones.

The gel melted quickly, suffusing the Ren'kari's battered shell with a gentle shine.

And as the minutes ticked by, Mon began to see a change. A flicker of movement, a twitch of exposed muscle. The pulsing of bioluminescence, growing stronger, steadier. A tiny bit brighter.

But Ar'asha didn't awaken.

Again they gathered by Olve's screens, Aster, Floyd, and Mon. The twins had gone upstairs to pack the lab and offices for evacuation. Everyone else was now somewhere in the eight-hour process of decompression, resting one landing or another of the long stairs going up-top.

"More aftershocks?" Mon asked Aster.

"None since the one when you were here," they said. "Knock wood." They rapped their temple.

Mon couldn't even pretend to smile. Aster's hand came to rest on her shoulder, a solid, steadying presence in the chill of the cargo cave. They must be freezing themselves, half sodden with water. Didn't even take their boots off.

"The gel is working," they said. "Doing its job. But it can only do so much. We need to find a way to shore up her system. Help her body heal itself."

Floyd seemed to have taken over the text screen. Mon came closer. The text was flowing even faster, four columns of it. Was Floyd memorizing medical texts?

"Chat rooms," Floyd said. Four different chats, scrolling at different speeds. Three were scrolling too fast for Mon to even catch a word. The one on the right was a little slower. Floyd pointed toward that one.

"Humans only. Others are mixed."

Olve joined them. "What's the consensus?"

"Four approaches," Aster said as they counted out the remaining gel packs. At Mon's look of surprise, they added, "I'm reading on the inside."

No wonder the synths could post so fast.

"Build a new exoskeleton," Floyd said. "No problem."

"But we don't know that she can't do that herself," Olve argued. "Some shrimp shed their shells and make new ones. Maybe we can stimulate her to do that."

Floyd glared at Olve. "Ask your friends."

Olve withered. "They refuse to talk about Ren'kari physiology." He looked over at Ar'asha. "I think they're scared. They don't want us to know too much about them."

The wasting disease.

Maybe they all had it.

Of course they wouldn't want to admit it.

Shitheads.

"And they'd let a girl die because of it?" Mon said.

"Wouldn't you?" Olve turned on her. He glared, but the look lost its effectiveness as he swayed on his feet. "When the fate of your species relies on everyone being afraid of you?"

"Maybe they should rely on something else," Mon shot back. "Like cooperation. Mutual benefit."

"Focus," Aster said. "Here are the options. Build her a new exoskeleton."

"Foreign objects," Floyd said. "Often rejected."

"Build her a set of braces so she can reform a skeleton on her own," Aster continued. "Like leg braces, when someone has broken a bone."

"Need to keep changing them out, then," Olve said.

"Just keep slathering nutrient gel on her and hope that Ren'kari have a magic ability to heal. Or turn her upside down and fill the bottom of the box with gel. Just soak her in it."

"Ambassador says she's a goner," Olve said.

"Or do nothing!" Aster said, exasperated.

Mon left them to their argument. She had to make sure Ar'asha was still okay. Or, if not okay, alive.

She kicked her boots off and rolled her pant legs up. She couldn't step into the box—the cold water would leach all her warmth in minutes. But she could stand by the edge. Even sit.

Keep Ar'asha company.

The Ren'kari's arms swayed in the water. Mon traced her finger down the nearest one.

Its colors twitched. Even a little bit of orange, among the purples and blues.

A good sign?

Another tremor shook the cave. The first one since they'd gotten back. No one mentioned it.

They would all have to leave the base. It wasn't safe.

And go where? That new cave was a bust.

Was this what the Ren'kari wanted? Get rid of the nosy humans.

No, they needed the gel. They would find another suitable place for a human base.

Sometime. When they weren't having their own emergencies.

But they were so close to communicating in the Ren'kari's own modalities.

But then, wasn't that what the Ren'kari were afraid of? Or, if the Ren'kari were fully healthy, would conversation with the humans be more palatable?

She couldn't solve this. It wasn't even her problem.

But Ar'asha was.

As she traced a finger down Ar'asha's arm again, Mon's belly rumbled. What time was it, even? She had no time to go find something to eat. Maybe she should try that nutrient gel. It smelled nice enough, but the pasty consistency did not appeal.

The arm under Mon's finger twitched. Physically, not just its light show.

And Ar'asha's eyes had gained some sparkle.

Mon finger-spelled Ar'asha's name with her hand against the girl's arm.

Another arm reached over, fingerspelling "Mon."

Ar'asha's whole body shivered. The argument behind Mon suddenly ceased.

Her eyes brightening. Ar'asha tried to move. Her arms reached around the vee braces as if they would push her body off the table.

"Stop!" Mon signed. "Your back is broken."

Ar'asha froze. She slowly unwrapped her arms from the braces. She reached up two arms to touch her back. When they touched a wound, her blinking changed to yellow-red. The gel must have some numbing property.

Good thing.

Aster rushed over.

"Ask how we can help her?"

Mon shook her head. "Something simpler."

"Ask her if she can regrow her skeleton."

Mon did so.

Ar'asha took a moment to answer. And another. Her signing arms lifted, and then dropped down again.

"Go through choices," Aster prodded.

Mon tried to think how to make it simple.

"We can make you a new shell," she signed.

"No," came back. "Need flexible."

"Make temporary support?" Mon tried. "Grow new shell, then take supports off."

"Maybe."

"What need?"

"Green gel. Time. Hope."

Mon translated for Aster.

They snorted.

"We have two of the three."

Chapter Twenty-Four

The next day Ar'asha hadn't stirred. But the patterns of her colors looked a little better, a little more intentional.

Or Mon was just lying to herself.

In the dim light of the cargo cave's night cycle, Mon re-wet the soggy blanket she had draped over Ar'asha. No one was sure how long Ren'kari could go without full immersion, and Mon was taking no chances.

The girl had made it through the night.

Mon had paced the cargo cave for hours. Each circuit, she checked on Ar'asha, draped over her special sawhorse-table half under water in that recycled-airlock of an emergency room.

Then she paced the rest of the steep room, fretting over every possible way things could go wrong. The most worrisome thing was the girl's failure to maintain consciousness. How could staying knocked out possibly serve her in the wilds of the ocean? Maybe Ren'kari burrowed when they were hurt, hiding until they healed? Maybe Ar'asha was too far gone, and Mon and the rest were just lying to themselves about it?

At the thought, the soles of her boots slammed against the gray stone floor.

She pulled her sweater tightly around her, stretching it unconscionably. Heather would tease her about destroying her gift in such a short time.

She wished Heather was here, with her energy, her curiosity, her smarts. Mon lifted her wrist to ping the girl—the young woman—before she thought better of it. It was the middle of the night on Arkhide.

She sent Heather a delayed message, timed to arrive at a reasonable hour of the morning. *Your sweater is a lifesaver, thanks. If you have time, check in on the Elders' chats. Any ideas?*

The far side of the pool, where the rovers were, and the workshop wall, where the tools hung on display along the wall, were perfectly tidy. Floyd's domains.

The near side of the pool, with the two tables of medical supplies and the printer, and the path from the elevators to the gel-mixing room were organized adequately, but nowhere near as precisely. And their dominant colors were blue and white, not shades of gray and rose.

Mon was pretty sure she could build a diorama of the entire cargo cave by now. Who knew she'd be spending so much time here?

Another small aftershock roiled the pool, splashing water on the edge. But the shocks today were tiny compared to the one that had bowled her over yesterday.

Finally Aster had made her sit in a reclining folding chair they'd found, and Mon had crashed asleep. Four hours later, she wasn't sure her feet would ever really get warm again.

But it was showtime, and she was up.

"They're here," Aster said.

In the morning-lit cargo cave, the bright ER lights still off in case they bothered Ar'asha, Mon stood with Aster and Floyd in front of the two big floating screens. One screen showed the flow of text conversation on the chats, the Arkhideans up-top trying to figure ways to help heal the Ren'kari.

The other screen gave a live view of the confrontation starting just above them, in Olve's lab.

Mon forgot how the cargo cave's damp chill had seeped into her bones, how thirsty she was in this room full of salty water. All her attention was on the screen. On the Ren'kari ambassador, facing off against Olve.

Olve, who had not slept in more than a day. Who probably hadn't eaten, since no one had remembered to remind him. Who, according to Aster, was losing his respect for the Ren'kari. Who was starting to distrust them.

On the screen, the view was Olve's back and the ambassador's front. The weirdly placed jewelry along the ambassador's exoskeleton glinted in the spotlights. Their bioluminescent patterns pulsed with agitation. But their lower limbs were, as always, placed gracefully beneath them.

Olve stood his ground, his shoulders stiff, his signs sharp and precise.

Next to Mon in the cave, Aster and Floyd were equally tense, their faces etched with worry. Floyd's pink-tipped fingers twitched, as if itching to intervene, while all of Aster's arms hugged their chest. Mon's hands were fisted, and jammed deep in the pockets of her wrinkled, musty coveralls.

Olve and the ambassador began with the usual greeting forms, a series of bows and weaves that could look friendly but today absolutely did not.

Mon strained to pick up every nuance of the conversation. The Listening device on the table behind Olve was broadcasting clearly, and the ambassador was not hard to read. The discordant overtones of their speech made her shoulders go rigid. She could sense the weight of their anger, the pressure of their resentment through their words.

"Good news," the ambassador signed, their movements stiff and formal. "The earthquakes here will subside. The activity is moving down the south fissure, not the north."

Aster let out a long breath. They touched their temple, a sign that they were communicating in-mind. Probably sending the news to everybody up and down the stairwell, saying they could come back to base.

But the relief was short-lived. Olve's hands flew in a flurry of signs. He signed with such force that the moves forced him to take a step back.

"How do we know you're telling the truth?" he said. "How do we know you're not just trying to keep the green gel flowing, no matter the risk to us?"

Mon's stomach clenched.

"Wow," Floyd said.

Olve's words were a slap in the face, a blatant accusation that cut through the thin veneer of diplomacy. The ambassador's patterns flared yellow, their anger palpable even without the clanking overtones.

"We would not endanger you," they signed, their movements sharp and precise. "We are..." They paused. Olve set his hands on his hips.

"Partners," the ambassador said.

Partners. The word hung in the air, heavy with implication. Did the Ren'kari even understand the word the way the Arkhideans did?

What kind of partnership was this, built on secrets and mistrust? How could they forge a true alliance when they knew so little about each other's worlds?

Floyd tapped the image of the ambassador. "Not happy," they said. "Look at that flash." She pulled two NutriBars out of the side pocket of her lilac coveralls and handed one to Mon.

Mon took it, nodding, her gaze fixed on the screen. She could see the tension in every line of the ambassador's body, the way their legs coiled and uncoiled beneath them. Roiling.

"Olve," Aster said, a whole world in one name. "Sending text message: Stay calm. Cooperate." They sighed. "We can fight about it later."

On the screen, Olve glanced down and to the right, reading the message through his comms implant. He shook his head. For a moment, Mon thought he might ignore the warning, his pride and frustration getting the better of him.

But then he took a deep breath, his shoulders easing.

"I apologize," he signed to the ambassador, his movements more measured. "We are grateful for your warning."

The ambassador's colors shifted, the angry yellow reds fading to a more neutral blue. "See that you remember it," they signed, their overtones still sharp. "We have much to discuss."

Good sign. Mon opened the wrapper on her protein bar and took a bite. Vanilla, not the worst.

So she missed the moment the ambassador's luminescence changed from a vibrant spectrum of colors to almost entirely blood red. But she heard the wailing overtones.

"You ventured too close to our city," the ambassador signed, their movements sharp and jagged. "You had no right, no permission."

Olve's shoulders shot up to nearly his ears.

"We meant no harm," he signed back, his gestures first deliberate and then getting a little messy. "We were only seeking shelter, a place of safety from the earthquakes."

The ambassador's patterns flashed a brilliant, searing white, the color of hot metal.

"Safety?" they signed, their overtones mocking. "And how did that go?"

Shit. They knew about the monster eels.

"We didn't know," Olve signed. "If we had known, we would never have entered its territory. If you had told us when we asked about it."

The ambassador's patterns dimmed, the red fading to a dull, pulsing orange.

"We did warn you," they signed, their movements curt.

"You said the site wouldn't suit," Olve pushed on. "But it would. Without the giant worm."

"You should listen to us," the ambassador said, using the form of "us" that means "your betters."

Mon hissed out a breath, glaring at the screen. Her fingers twitched to sign a response of her own. A non-diplomatic response.

How dare the ambassador lecture them about communication, about trust, when they had been so quick to dismiss Ar'asha's life as worthless?

On the screen, Olve wiped that part of the conversation away with a wide swipe of his arm. Cool as the underside of a pillow. Even the ambassador pulsed a tone of wary respect.

"We have a more pressing concern," Olve signed.

The ambassador's patterns shifted, the orange fading to a muted yellow. They said nothing, waiting for Olve to make his move.

Olve took a deep breath, his chest rising and falling with the effort of it.

"Ar'asha," he signed, his movements slow with the need to spell each letter. "How can we help her?"

The ambassador's exoskeleton flared a diamond-bright white. Shock? Their arms coiled and uncoiled, their movements jerky and agitated. Their overtones disappeared.

"The girl," they signed, their gestures choppy. "She lives?"

Olve nodded and then signed yes. "We think she will heal. With your help."

The ambassador's patterns shifted, the white fading to a deep, pulsing dark red shot through with streaks of purple-black.

"Unacceptable," they signed, their movements jagged and erratic. "Her fate is not yours to decide. She belongs to us. To the People."

Mon's heart clenched, a sudden, icy feeling of dread washing over her. She glanced at Aster and Floyd, saw the same horrified realization etched onto their faces.

They had known that the Ren'kari would not be pleased by their intervention, by their decision to save Ar'asha's life. But to see the depth of the ambassador's anger, the fury that radiated from their body. Terrifying.

On the screen, Olve wasn't giving in. "With all due respect, Ambassador, we cannot simply hand her over to you. Not when we can't be sure you will help her."

The ambassador's patterns flashed white again, a star going supernova. The overtones were back, like broken bugles.

"You dare to defy us? You dare to question our authority?"

Olve stood his ground, his hands steady and sure as he signed his response.

"We dare to do what is right," he signed. "We dare to value the life of one of your own, even when you would cast her aside."

"Yeah!" said Floyd. "Our boy, stepping up!"

"Wait for it," Aster said.

The ambassador went still. They drew nearer to the window, looming over Olve.

"It is a condition of your residence on this planet that you do not interfere with the People."

Olve dropped his arms to his sides but stood his ground.

"Need some help, here," popped up on Mon's wristcom. Aster and Floyd must have received the message directly.

"Ask him to clarify," Aster whispered. "He can't mean they would revoke our permission to stay on Arkhide."

"Let them try," Floyd growled, her pink-tipped fingers clenched into fists. "Got leverage now. They need our green gel as much as we need their goodwill."

In the lab, Olve started to sign again.

"Help me understand," he said. "You would banish us from the planet merely because we refuse to murder one of the People?"

That was it for the ambassador.

"We're done," they signed. They shot off the narrow shelf outside the lab window.

Headed down. Not to the left.

"Shit," Aster said. "They're coming down here."

Chapter Twenty-Five

The ambassador was coming. As soon Mon saw them on the video screen dropping straight down from the lab instead of off to the left, she knew.

Straight for the cargo cave.

Coming for Ar'asha.

And they were mad. Blaring mad. Not even trying to mask their tones, just blasting them out.

Well, they weren't going to get her.

Aster and Floyd were already in motion. Aster ran toward the transparent box that was Ar'asha's patchwork hospital room. They stepped down, into the water that filled half the room, and pushed toward the outer door. They pulled the door closed, locked it, and set the emergency bar across it.

Then they pulled out their diving knife.

Floyd was over by the rovers, doing something to a control panel. A sharp crack, and the top of the moon pool's water buzzed with electricity.

It didn't stop the Ren'kari ambassador.

The ambassador burst through the electric barrier with such force their whole body left the water. They landed on their back legs on the inner end of the pool. Their crystalline exoskeleton flashed reds and oranges. Mon almost couldn't think, the Ren'kari was so loud.

They scanned the room, saw Mon and Aster, saw the water-box-room five meters away. Popped with a new pattern oranges and reds.

Beelined for Ar'asha.

On land, the ambassador moved with a loping speed that defied belief. Their arms and legs propelled them as if the air were water.

Floyd was running back from the rover area, coming from behind the ambassador but not even matching speed with them.

Mon threw herself in front of the door to the little room. Behind her she heard Aster grunt as they pulled the door closed. Now they were closed in with Ar'asha.

Aster could've given her the knife first. Mon had nothing in her pockets but a spare wristcom battery and a used NutriBar wrapper.

The ambassador barreled right at her. Did they think they could mow her down?

Good luck.

At the last minute, Mon stepped toward them, past the edge of the little room and a bit to the side. Opening a lane for them.

As they passed, Mon hip-checked them, hard.

Right into the pool.

Served them right.

They were out of the water almost before they went into it.

Mon couldn't believe it.

Floyd was only a few steps away from the ambassador now. Still not fast enough.

This time, the ambassador used their reach. They whipped two arms around Mon's shoulders. They jerked her forward, off-balance, and then flung her into the water.

She knew the Ren'kari were strong, but wow.

Mon knew she couldn't stop the fall. She took in a breath and prepared for the shock.

Double shock. The coating of electricity Floyd had laid on the pool's water burned her skin just before the icy water froze it.

Bloody hells.

The incredible jump in pressure popped her eardrums and stung her all over. It wouldn't crush her right away, thanks to the special mixture of air down here. Less nitrogen, so less nitrogen narcosis. But she couldn't afford to be in here long.

She had to get out, now.

She kicked to the side of the pool. Reached a hand up to grab the edge.

The shock of electricity against her wrist pushed the rest of the air out of her lungs. Mon pulled the hand back under.

Now that she was wet, the current could be deadly.

Floyd must be going back to turn the electricity off. It wouldn't take them long. She had enough time.

She had no air. Her chest—her lungs—felt crushed. Her heart was pumping so hard her body would have been on fire if it was in the air. In the pool, she was ice.

Shadows passed in front of her. Someone short and quiet.

Someone taller. Louder.

The ambassador. They hadn't made it to the room yet. And Floyd. So she wasn't going to be able to turn the power off.

So be it.

Mon kicked, trying to tread just under the surface of the water. But she couldn't feel her feet. She couldn't be sure she wouldn't get too close to the current along the surface.

Her thoughts were going fuzzy. So cold.

Think.

She'd been in danger before, and alone.

Here she had people. They would help her.

But they needed to help Ar'asha first.

Ice was creeping up her bones, aiming for her heart.

She was going to have to risk the electric field.

Mon got as close to the wall of the pool as possible. She couldn't be slow about it. Do it the Ren'kari way: whole body thrust.

Mon kicked as hard as she could—no use saving energy. Her shoulders screamed as they left the water. But her hands got hold of the edge. Another kick, another scream, and she was stretched along the edge of the pool. Writhing. But on the right side. The side with air.

No time for rest. She rolled away from the pool and onto her hands and knees. She blinked water out of her eyes. Shook it out of her ears. Her eardrums popped, hard. Her nose was bleeding. Her vision was still blurry. Her eyes must have gotten squeezed out of whack.

"Look out!"

Floyd. In front of her. In front of Ar'asha's room.

So where was the ambassador?

Right behind her, and coming fast. Floyd must have gotten them into the water again, and they came up in the same spot as before.

Now they would have to mow down both Mon and Floyd to get to Ar'asha.

The ambassador's lights pulsed more orange than red. The electric shocks must be taking something out of them.

Mon pushed up with to her numb legs, staggering toward Floyd. Floyd grabbed her shoulder—her grip burned—and pulled Mon behind her.

But the ambassador wasn't coming for them anymore. They had catapulted themself onto the top of the box, landing hard.

Must have thought the box had no top—joke on them.

The box shuddered. It tipped maybe ten degrees, maybe twenty, and then tipped back.

Floyd grabbed at a swirling arm, or was it a leg? The ambassador whipped an arm across Floyd's face, stunning her back two steps.

The ambassador looked down. Their gaze seemed to lock with Aster's. The synth had their upper arms, one with the knife, facing the Ren'kari. Their lower arms were supporting Ar'asha in case the box moved again.

The ambassador froze. Their arms and legs stilled. The colors along them suddenly flashed all colors, and then settled into blues and greens.

Mon followed their gaze.

Her eyes widened in shock.

Chapter Twenty-Six

The ambassador, stock-still on top of the transparent room Ar'asha was resting in, appeared mesmerized. Their colors slowed; their overtones dropped to a hum.

The soggy towel had slipped off Ar'asha's back. Her exoskeleton was healing, the jagged cracks and fissures knitting together almost in front of their eyes. The flexible carbon struts that Floyd had so carefully placed just last night were doing their job, guiding the regrowth of the siliconate shell.

But it was the color of the new growth that stole Mon's breath. That sent a thrill of disbelief and wonder through her nerves.

It was clear. As transparent as the ambassador's own shell.

The implications hit Mon like a physical blow, her mind reeling. The disease that plagued the Ren'kari, the wasting that Ar'asha had hinted at... it was gone.

Healed.

Cured?

The ambassador's patterns shifted, cycling through confusion, wonder, fear, and deep, pulsing anger. Their overtones screamed.

They looked at Mon. "What have you done?" they signed.

Mon shook her head. "We didn't do this," she signed. "She did."

Mon pointed to Ar'asha. "She trusted us, and we trusted her. And look what's happened."

The ambassador's gaze flicked to Ar'asha, to the clear, shimmering expanse of her already half-healed exoskeleton. Their patterns did not calm.

Then, with a suddenness that made Mon flinch, the ambassador reached up and tore one of the shiny metal ornaments from their own shell.

Beneath the ornament, the ambassador's shell was dull, the same sickly gray as Ar'asha's.

The wasting, laid bare for all to see.

"It's chronic," they signed. Their overtones softened, saddened. "You do not understand," they signed. "The cost of your actions, the price we will all pay…"

Ar'asha had hinted at this before, at a deeper problem within the Ren'kari culture. But to hear it confirmed by the ambassador themselves. Mon's breath caught, her sea-blurry eyes widened with sudden realization.

"You are all affected?" she signed.

The Ren'kari might die.

They might all die.

"The disease is chronic," the ambassador signed, their gestures heavy. "The distribution of the cure is not equal. You have tipped the balance by healing a less desirable among us."

Mon shoved her hair back from her face, pushing cold water down her back in the process.

"How were we supposed to know she was undesirable?" she said. "She was willing to talk with us."

"That's how," the ambassador signed. "Talking to the humans is not an honor."

"The weakening is our weakness, our shame," they continued. "The rot that eats at the very heart of our society. This green gel—it is not just a luxury, or a trade item. It is critical."

How lowering it must be, for such a private people. Mon could see it now. The Ren'kari's insistence on secrecy, their desperate need for green gel production to be on time, continual. Their refusal to interact in with the Arkhideans in any but the most distant ways.

"Using so much gel to heal this one is a waste," they signed at last, their movements heavy with resignation. "Not when so many more of our people are in need."

Mon's heart ached, a deep, wrenching pain that stole her breath. She understood the ambassador's desperation now, the terrible burden of responsibility they carried.

"We will find a way," she signed. "We will use what we have learned from Ar'asha. Work together to find a lasting solution for your people. But we will not hand her over to an uncertain fate."

The ambassador's patterns flickered, a brief flash of something like doubt amidst the rage.

"You cannot understand," they signed, their gestures heavy, their overtones turning bitter. "You are not Ren'kari. You do not bear the weight of our history, our shame."

"Then help us understand," she signed, her movements fierce and emphatic.

At that moment, Olve burst into the room, his eyes wide at the sight before him. "What's going on? Is Ar'asha...?"

Mon quickly explained aloud, gesturing to Ar'asha's healing exoskeleton.

Olve's gaze snapped to the ambassador. He nodded.

He had this answer ready.

"That's not how it is with us," he signed to the ambassador and said aloud. "Humans and synthetic humans are all about cooperation. Right now, hundreds of us are studying what we've learned from Ar'asha. We want to find a permanent cure, not just a treatment."

"Help us find a way to heal your people, to end this suffering," Olve continued. "We are not your enemies, Ambassador. We won't attack you. Our people gain from knowing your people."

The ambassador's patterns dimmed, the angry reds and oranges fading to a dull, pulsing gray. They seemed to deflate, their arms curling in on themselves in a gesture of defeat and exhaustion.

"I do not know if that is possible," they signed, their movements slow and hesitant. "Not all the People agree about the topsiders. Some never wanted you. For them to work together with you? It might be impossible."

But their overtones suggested hope.

"We can only try," Mon signed. "What do you think?"

The ambassador was still for a long moment, their patterns cycling through the blues and oranges of contemplation. Then their overtones changed. Brightened, somehow.

"Open the door?" they signed. "I will not harm her."

Mon looked at Olve. Olve nodded to Aster, who had put their knife away long ago.

Aster unblocked the inner door and opened it. The scent of wet blanket, burnt-grass gel, and Ren'kari wafted out.

Slowly, the ambassador reached an arm down. They brushed their three fingers along Ar'asha's healing exoskeleton. The colors along their arm pulsed quickly and then settled into a slow rhythm. Like a lullaby.

"This one is my offspring," they signed with two other arms. "My only. She was born early, and weakened quickly. I could not show favor."

They pulled the lullaby arm away from their daughter for a moment. When they brought it back, they lay their discarded jewel on one of the braces holding Ar'asha's back in place. The arm returned to playing its lullaby.

"I cannot even now. Not just for her. I serve all the People."

They kept up the lullaby for another minute, and then pulled the arm away.

"We have not found a cure," the ambassador signed. "It has been hundreds of years. All my memory."

It wasn't a weakness to need medicine. Up-top, at least. In the ocean, Mon wasn't so sure.

"I will return to my conclave," the ambassador signed, "and convey your offer, and your intentions. I do not hope, but I am willing to try."

"I leave the child with you."

Chapter Twenty-Seven

Three days after all the excitement, everyone had healed.

Mon watched, wincing, as Floyd removed the last three of the braces that had held Ar'asha's exoskeleton together. Ar'asha said there was no pain, but that sucking-popping sound as the pieces pulled away felt too much like ripping off a scab for Mon's liking.

The young Ren'kari had woken up early this morning. As the cargo cave's lights were mimicking dawn. Ar'asha popped to life if she were waking up from a nap.

"Best to sleep," she signed about her long rest. "If doesn't heal, you just stay asleep."

Mon, who had not been able to sleep for the entire five hours she'd had to spend in the hyperbaric chamber, getting re-pressurized after her unplanned dip in the pool, tried to picture it. Aster said she was lucky all she had was a busted ear drum and deep-bruised lungs. "Don't ever do that again," they warned—and then joked that she had won "First in Pool" bragging rights.

Ar'asha was delighted with the recycled airlock that had been her emergency room for half a week. She'd spent the morning opening and closing the doors from both sides. Once she climbed on top to rest and, apparently, check out the view. She didn't remember the airlock in the rover, the one that had brought her, cocooned in a net, back to the cargo cave. She wanted to try the airlock up in the lab next.

She wasn't as fond of the sawhorse they had draped her over in lieu of a bed. Apparently, Ren'kari curl up in corners or under things when they sleep.

And she didn't remember her parent—the ambassador!— coming to visit. Not that first, eventful time, nor the second, yesterday.

But today she was fully alive, and curious.

And wriggling, her luminescence reflecting her impatience to be off the hated sawhorse that was her emergency room's bed. Her patterns pulsed steady, a vibrant glow, no longer the erratic flashes of earlier days.

Floyd stood in the frigid water under the sawhorse as if it were a warm bath. As she pulled away each piece of the brace, she handed it through the poolside door of the room to Mon. They didn't feel at all like scabs, but smooth curved carbon. The braces carried only a trace of burnt summer grass from their green-gel coating.

Floyd pulled away the last brace, along the center of Ar'asha's back.

The once-shattered shell now shimmered crystalline clear. The jagged cracks and missing chips had smoothed into translucent planes that caught the light like a prism.

That green gel was good.

Ar'asha wriggled her body a bit, her luminescence dancing, and then looked at Floyd.

"Okay?" she signed.

"What's the sign for perfect?" Floyd asked Mon. Mon made the sign, and Floyd copied it. Both of them had pink-tipped nails now. Floyd had suggested a nail party the second day into Mon's bedside —poolside—vigil. Mon still wasn't used to it.

Ar'asha squealed, overtones in the human-hearing range. Floyd glanced at Mon in surprise.

"That's an overtone," Mon confirmed. "The range starts just at the limits of normal human hearing."

"Screechy," Floyd said.

"You have no idea." But Floyd would, soon, along with everyone else. Heather said she had enough—"way enough"— samples of the sounds to program an effective block to add to their Listener-noise canceling headphones.

But they wanted something more, this time. A way to produce the sounds, and understand them. Neither Mon nor Heather had considered that important before, but it was critical now. To decode the mood, the emphasis, maybe even the tense, of the Ren'kari language.

Heather could do it, Mon had no doubt. Floyd was already working on controllable light panels that could mimic the color range of their communications. Someday Floyd—everyone— would be able to say "perfect" in Ren'kari.

Ar'asha slid off the sawhorse-bed on the same side as Floyd, who gave her arm a quick stroke. They'd found that touch seemed to calm Ar'asha, and didn't harm human or synthetic human skin. Humans and Ren'kari shared that one thing in common, at least.

Ar'asha slid four of her arms around the sawhorse bed and tugged. It lifted off the floor of the transparent box easily. Heavy composite carbonate, it hadn't needed to be hard-fixed. Ar'asha slid it past Floyd. Once it passed Floyd, Ar'asha flung it into the water of the moon pool.

Then she turned around to look at them, eyes a silver whirl. Defiant.

Floyd laughed. And then quickly sobered.

"Tell her the humans aren't supposed to pollute the waters," she said to Mon.

"I did it," Ar'asha signed. "Not humans." She looked back, into the water. "I'll go get it later."

She launched herself into the water, but rather than go deep she headed for the short shelf at the edge of the inner side of the pool. Her favorite chat-spot.

Floyd had finished her Listener device 2.0, just as good as Heather's, with more-expensive component, and waterproof to boot. It sat on a short packing box near Ar'asha, along with the comms tablets and the piece of jewelry the ambassador had left. Now they could Listen both here and up at the lab.

Floyd went back to that ever-cascading chat-room screen, now set against her workshop wall. The Arkhideans had set up a contest for who could find a better delivery system for the gel, and Floyd was betting on pills. She already had a dozen failed prototypes, and counting.

Mon went to sit by Ar'asha, who had perched on the pool shelf expectantly.

"Don't you want to swim?" she asked the girl. "Stretch your legs?"

"Tell me what happened," Ar'asha said.

"When you were injured?" Mon had told the girl before, but maybe Ar'asha had been too injured to remember.

"No." Ar'asha picked up the jewel—Mon was going to call it a broach, whatever—and brought it close to her chest. "When the ambassador was here."

Mon recounted the conversation, the attack, the change of heart.

"So you know," Ar'asha said. A flicker in her eyes reminded Mon of dappled shadows on leaves. Her scent, a summer field of sweet corn.

"That they are your parent? Yes."

Ar'asha rolled the broach from arm to arm. Clapping onto it with one trio of fingers, handing it off to another trio, up and down her torso. Her colors started to fade, much like they were when Mon first met her.

"What's wrong?" Mon said.

Ar'asha's arms twisted, her patterns cycling through shades of blue and gray.

"I won't be welcome anymore," she signed, her gestures slow. "My voice, my..." she hesitated as if searching for the word. She looked over to the table, to the tablets. But she didn't reach for them.

"My shell, it's changed."

"The color, you mean."

"Color. Also..." Again she searched for the word. What else would an improved exoskeleton change?

"Your voice," Mon said. Not the right word, but they hadn't found one better yet. She would just pick one. "Your overtones."

"Yes. I don't sound like myself anymore. They will be confused. And angry."

Too bad. Mon had no sympathy for the Ren'kari hierarchs, or whatever they were.

Gel-hoarders.

But for Ar'asha, her heart ached. Mon knew all too well the fear of being an outsider, of not belonging in the place you once called home.

The reality of it.

Bullheaded Ren'kari politics.

"You have us," she signed, her movements fierce and emphatic.

"You have a place here. We care about you. We want you happy. We'll figure something out."

Ar'asha's glittery eyes brightened. Her patterns bloomed brighter. She reached a hand out. Mon lifted her hand. Ar'asha wrapped her warm arm around Mon's wrist.

So gentle. So strong.

At the sound of footsteps echoing through the cargo bay, Mon turned around.

Olve, his face a mixture of excitement and concern. He approached the pair, his eyes widening as he took in the sight of Ar'asha's healed exoskeleton.

"Incredible," he signed. "Ar'asha, you look radiant. How do you feel?"

"Better," she signed. "Can I stay?"

Olve squatted down to their level. His brow furrowed, his gaze darting between Ar'asha and Mon.

"What does she mean?" he said aloud. "Of course you're welcome here, Ar'asha." he signed.

Mon spoke and signed. "She's worried about returning to her city, about how her people will react to her new appearance. It is a sign of changed status, but maybe they'll think she hasn't earned it, somehow?"

Olve's gaze went hard. He looked much better, as well. Must have slept—and listened to Aster's nagging him to eat.

He turned to face Ar'asha, his signs big and clear. "Stay here. With us. We can make a room for you, off the observation deck. You'll have privacy, but also the company of those who care for you."

Ar'asha's patterns flickered, surprise in her luminescent display but doubt scratching along her overtones.

"True?" she signed, her movement hesitant.

"True," Olve replied, his gestures emphatic. "Think of the

opportunities. You can help us learn Listener sounds, teach us more about your language and culture. We have so much to learn from each other."

Ar'asha considered Olve's words, her arms twining over and over. Still playing with that broach.

"There is plankton here," she signed. "Good plankton. And silver fish."

Olve's gaze went opaque a moment. Sending a message.

Floyd bustled over.

"No problem!" she said. She grinned at Ar'asha. "Talk for me?" she asked Mon.

Floyd plopped to a seat directly in front of Ar'asha, nearly toppling the little table. "You like the box, right?" She pointed toward the transparent box half-filled with the sea and now empty of the apparently despised table-bed. "We can use that."

Ar'asha followed Floyd's gesture, saw Mon's translation, and squealed.

"Even I heard that one," Olve said.

Mon marveled at the change in Olve. The hard-driven and single-minded researcher now offering compassion and under-standing to a being he had once viewed as little more than a test subject.

"Looks like we'll need to set up a classroom, too," Mon signed, her movements teasing. "Professor Ar'asha, teaching Talk like the People 101."

Olve grinned. "I'll be your first student," he signed. "And I have a feeling there will be many more."

Chapter Twenty-Eight

Mon stood by the large observation windows in Olve's lab, her gaze drawn to the dark expanse of the ocean beyond. Her mind, to a certain set of overtones, coming from the left.

Olve, beside her, and Ar'asha on the other side of the window, pored over a holographic blueprint between them, their faces reflecting by the soft blue glow of the projected image.

"This could work," Olve signed. Ar'asha didn't sound as sure.

They'd already decided that the transparent airlock they'd used as an emergency room would serve as an apartment for the Ren'kari. But she didn't want the room here, on the metal deck jutting out into the water. She wanted it underneath the shelf.

For privacy.

Who could blame her?

"Okay," Olve signed. "Floyd says plenty of room." He tapped the blue outline of the boxy room on the blueprint and dragged it underneath the outline of the shelf.

Outside, Ar'asha made a circle motion with an arm. "Turn, so both doors can open."

The box fit in snug, the front-and-back doors now left-and-right-side-doors.

At last, agreement.

And just in time.

The Ren'kari ambassador glided into view, their clear silicon exoskeleton shimmering with a kaleidoscope of colors. And no jewelry. They must be getting more of the green gel. The People must have changed how they distributed it.

Ar'asha quickly dropped out of sight under the deck.

"Ambassador!" Olve signed. Both he and Mon performed the expected greeting. "Your timing is perfect," Olve said. "The shipment is ready." Negotiations had started about programming drones to deliver the kegs and return the empty ones. The Ren'kari wanted to wait, to build a surplus before experimenting with a system that might lose or damage the deliveries.

The ambassador settled gracefully, but kept looking down. Their overtones weren't as muted as usual—actually, really loud—but Mon was getting better at blocking the overwhelm.

The ambassador turned to Mon and Olve, their patterns pulsing with a deep, resonant blue. "I owe you a debt that cannot be repaid," they signed, their gestures formal. "You have done more than save my child's life. You have opened the door to a new future, a new way of being."

Olve nearly vibrated out of his skin. "Does that mean your conclave has agreed to work together with us? Already?"

The ambassador nodded in a human way, their patterns settling into a deep blues and oranges.

"It may be that we have had... clues... about a cure," they said. "It may be that we have had these clues for... a long time. It may be that this information was not shared among all the People."

Wow. It may be that there were some hot words being exchanged down in Ren'kari town this week.

"I have a memory device that can work with your tablet," the ambassador signed.

Olve nearly tripped, he ran so fast to the storage area to fetch the tablets. The Ren'kari had never shared such information.

The Ren'kari had never, ever, showed them any of their technology.

The ambassador's gaze followed Olve's progress. Once Olve set the tablet into the lab's airlock, it would take another full minute to fill with water before the ambassador could fetch it.

As Olve stepped into the storage area, the ambassador slid off the platform, ducking underneath.

Mon couldn't see them, or Ar'asha, who must still be there. But she could see the flickers of colors flashing rapidly in the reflection of floating plankton. And she heard when the two Ren'kari's overtones came into harmony.

Another new aspect of the Ren'kari language. Was it kinship? Empathy? Mon wasn't about to ask them today.

Let them enjoy each other in peace.

Immediately when the clank of the airlock signaled it had filled, the ambassador was in front of it, pressing the panel to open the outer door. By the time Olve had looked up from synching the tablets, the Ren'kari was in front of him, settled, as if they'd never left.

They pulled out a green net bag from somewhere near their shell. The pearl-shaped object they took out somehow morphed into a form that fit into the bigger data port on the tablet.

"Sweet waters," Olve whispered as he watched the data transfer. "The data packet is huge. It will take months just to scan."

"Nah, as Aster would say," Mon said. "Just throw it on the chat boards. They'll devour it in a day."

Olve chuckled. "Got that right. As Floyd would say." He looked up, to the ambassador.

"Thank you for this," he signed. "We will collect and share all we have, next time. If I put our information in the tablet, can your device pull it out?" Under his breath, he said, "Or you could just leave the device."

"Understood," the ambassador said.

Olve and Mon shared a glance. What, exactly, had the ambassador understood?

"One more thing," Olve signed. "We have offered shelter to the young Ren'kari, Ar'asha."

"Agree," the ambassador said. "It would not do for her to be seen in her present state. In a year, when others before her have completed their transformation, she will be accepted."

"She can be a bridge between our peoples," Olve signed.

"One that has been a long time coming," agreed the ambassador.

Chapter Twenty-Nine

M on sat cross-legged on her bed, Heather's nubbly soft sweater wrapped around her, waiting for her friend to answer her call. They were hologramming it, so Mon checked the room: lights bright enough, background dull enough.

She'd not been in this room much in the past—what was it, only a week? Beyond the small pile of dirty socks in the corner hidden in the corner behind the door, there wasn't much of Mon here.

She'd have to do something about that.

As Heather's face and torso shimmered into view, Mon felt a rush of warmth and affection. And pride: The girl had been through so much, and had grown and changed so fast.

Not girl. Young woman.

"Mon!" Heather said, her grape-soda-tinted lips curving into a grin. "I can't believe it! You actually found another damsel in distress to rescue. All the way at the bottom of the ocean!"

Mon laughed. Hadn't thought of it that way.

"Guess it's just what I do," she said, striking a pose. "Seriously, though. Ar'asha... she's different. She's the rescuer—she might've saved her whole people."

Heather's expression softened, her gaze filled with understanding.

"I get it," she said, her voice gentle. "You never want to take the credit."

Mon frowned. That couldn't be true.

"Gotcha!" Heather crowed. She pumped her fists.

Mon faked a pout. "And I was going to give you some interesting news."

Heather's eyes widened, a glimmer of hope, of excitement, dancing in their depths. "Does that mean what I think it means?"

Mon grinned. "Olve said yes. We need your help. In person, not just on the chats."

Heather let out a squeal of delight. Her shape blurred as she bounced in her seat.

"Yes!" she said, her image settling down. "Floyd said best she could do would be next year. But I knew you could do better."

"Well, it did help that nobody else on the entire planet has the Listener skill."

"Except you."

"Even me," Mon said. "No, really. You're the analyst. You and Floyd can make this work. She's brilliant, too." Hard to believe she used to have to force herself not to shy away from synths. "Me and Ar'asha, we're the beta testers. You'll love Ar'asha."

"Ar'asha? That's how you say it?" Heather sighed. "Ar..ah..sha. Beautiful. Do they really have six arms? And four legs? And smell like sweet corn?"

Heather froze a moment, as if she were replaying their conversation. Then she perked up again.

"Wait. You're staying?"

"Heard it here first," Mon said. "They want both of us. Start packing your bags, kid." Oops, young woman. "Bring warm clothes. Lots of socks. And that grape drink, too. We've got none of that here."

"You won't be sorry," Heather burbled. "I'm gonna learn fast, and figure out the light board with Floyd. And Floyd said she was working on sound boards, too."

"Sounds like you've got a new best friend."

"I wish." Heather's exuberance dissipated like a balloon deflating. "What if she doesn't like me?"

Still a very young woman.

"You know what?" Mon said. "See if you can get some fancy nail polish to bring down. Floyd is really into bright red and pink. She painted parts of the sea rovers pink!"

Heather's mouth twisted in thought. "Does she need a sweater? My house mom made yours. She could make a pink one for Floyd. Send me her size?"

Mon was positive that Floyd never needed a sweater. And equally positive that the synthetic human would wear it every single time Heather came to visit.

"Perfect," Mon said. "And have her make one for you, too."

<hr>

As Mon stepped into the lab, she was struck by the change in the atmosphere. Gone was the tension that had soaked every square centimeter. In its place, calm. Camaraderie.

And the scent of the chili Aster had made for lunch.

Olve no longer spent his days hiding in his workshop castle. He leaned on a high stool next to the observation windows, his long fingers dancing across two big floating screens, explaining some complex data set to Ar'asha, on the other side of the window. They were the same height.

The young Ren'kari listened intently, her bioluminescent patterns pulsing steady. Her overtones were calm, if one could call a lower level of sawing steel calm.

"Mon!" Olve said, his face breaking into a smile as he noticed her. "Perfect timing. We were just discussing the new data from last night's gel simulations."

"Tell me all about it." She really hoped they wouldn't, but she soldiered on, marching to the window and making her face look studious. Later they could get into linguistics and the other good stuff.

Olve launched into an explanation, his hands moving in a mix of GSL and the pidgin they were creating with Ar'asha for unique Ren'kari-only terms. Olve looked like a new man. Or newly refurbished.

Gone was the single-minded obsession, the bitterness, the stubborn refusal to consider other perspectives. In its place was a cautious openness, a willingness to collaborate. To let others lead, once in a while.

Ar'asha, too, had grown in such a short time. No longer the frightened, uncertain youngster she had been when they first met, she now radiated a quiet confidence.

Mon managed to ask a couple of reasonable questions before the talk got too granular. Soon, the other two forgot all about her, barreling on with their analysis.

Mon gazed out the window, into the shimmering expanse of the underwater world beyond. The soft glow of the creatures that danced through the murky depths cast a mesmerizing light across the platform. The water dim, vast, and mysterious. Like space and not at all like.

The biggest puzzle of them all.

Also by Nicky Penttila

Cooperative Realm: Arkhide

Secrets of the Synths

Worlds Apart

Hidden Planet

The Listeners

The Elders of Arkhide

Cooperative Realm: Frankie

Cargo Trouble

Frankie Takes a Holiday

Frankie Takes a Dive

Historical Fiction

A Note of Scandal

An Untitled Lady

The Spanish Patriot

About the Author

Nicky Penttila wrote her first story, a Mayan murder mystery, in seventh grade. But then came gymnastics, math team, and boyfriends. Later came husband, car payments, and a sleep-depriving work schedule at newspapers across the country. Then came a second career as a science writer. But the fiction kept trickling out, a story here, a novella there, and finally, a real live novel. And she hasn't stopped.

Find more great reads at nickypenttila.com